RUT

Rut

A NOVEL BY

SCOTT PHILLIPS

CONCORD
FREE
PRESS

Published by Concord Free Press
152 Commonwealth Avenue
Concord, Massachusetts 01742
www.concordfreepress.com

ISBN 978-0-9817824-4-7

Designed by Chris DeFrancesco
www.alphabeticadesign.com

Printed in the United States by Recycled Paper Printing
www.recycledpaper.com

First edition limited to 3,000 numbered copies (see page 229)

In memory of David Thompson

1

HER WEEK'S SUPPLIES PURCHASED, Bridget walks the bicycle in lurching bumps over the shattered asphalt away from the center of the town of Gower until she reaches the ruin of an old commercial district glimpsed the week before, when she was too busy to take pictures.

The sidewalks are weedy and crumbling, the street devoid of inhabited homes or open businesses. An enormous sinkhole, eight feet wide at the center, breaks up the asphalt on Rattigan at Sixth, and there's another one half a block up. Some of the signs for restaurants and stores remain, though, and one long-defunct enterprise still contains some of its merchandise lined up on dusty shelves. The John Whitefeather Ghost Dance Gallery stands in between a former souvenir shop and the empty husk of an upscale women's clothing store. Inside hang framed posters of Navajo women, the pastel colors faded by the sun in varying degrees according to their distance from the cracked, grimy window. Bridget steps back into the street to frame it, adjusts the polarizer. As she sets up a dramatic wide shot of the storefront and interior, she hears a whiskey-deep voice lisping behind her.

"John Whitefeather wanted to be an Indian *so bad*." Bridget turns to face an ancient, tan woman whose slack skin hangs in folds from her face to well below the jawline. Her pronounced lisp seems due to whatever cosmetic procedure accounts for those pouty lips, so full and smooth and immobile. They look like they've been grafted onto her from a great-granddaughter, as do her breasts, far too large and unnaturally perky.

"So you knew this guy?"

"John was as white as they come. His real name was John Whitehall, but he told everybody he was part Cherokee and part Choctaw. And all that Navajo and Hopi stuff in there is bullshit. It was all Utes around here, but that Navajo crap was what the tourists wanted, so that's what he stocked. Grew his hair long in a pony tail and wore a beaded band around his forehead and talked about our mother the mountain 'n all that shit." The old woman shakes her head and fingers her regenerated golden hair, long and wavy and lustrous. Though her lips don't move much, when she speaks they separate far enough to reveal a set of perfectly straight and white teeth, also regenerated. "What an asshole."

"Weird how those posters are still up there after all this time," Bridget says.

"Nobody wants that shit anymore. Nobody around here, anyway."

"What happened to him?"

"Snorted himself out of business. Big. Old. Crankhead. That's how I knew him. We were crank buddies. I got off it when they came down on it so hard 'cause I was scared of jail, but John got taken away. Bet he died in the jug."

"Too bad."

"Shit, he was nothing to me. But you should've seen this place back in the day. Big stars used to come here to ski and fish and snort and screw. I did a threesome with Rod Stewart and that other dude, what's his fuck. You know, with the feathery hair? Sixty years or so back, just about, and my friend Tinnie blew three of the Eagles that same winter."

These mysterious names are plainly meant to impress, so Bridget pretends. "Whoa. Three of 'em, huh?"

"That's right, including that one who looked like some kind of Neanderfuck." She looks Bridget up and down. "You look like a partier. Should have been there."

"Yeah," Bridget says. "Can I take your picture?"

"Fuck no, bitch."

Without another word the old woman trundles away, sashaying her bony ass from side to side like the hot babe she must have been in her dissolute prime.

Reluctant still to head straight back to camp Bridget decides to explore. A woman she met on her grocery run the week before gave her a dubious tip about some frogs in a lake on her ranch, and she heads toward the property in question over a dirt and gravel county road that hasn't been maintained in decades. The bike bumps and jerks, her hands tight on the handlebars, arms stiff to keep the front wheel from flying off to the side.

Even so, she's happy to be away from camp even for an afternoon. Gower is the shittiest excuse for summer fieldwork ever, and she suspects career sabotage on the part of her boss, who's more or less openly sleeping with Bridget's rival, Jean Masterson. Consequently, Jean drew a plumy field assignment—a South American expedition in search of a rumored population of fantastically repugnant mammoth Surinam toads, their fully developed offspring erupting baseball-sized from honeycombed pockets in their mothers' backs. The toads are surely as imaginary as any re-emergent Colorado bullfrogs, but something of interest is bound to be lurking down there in the tropics, waiting to be written up by some intrepid young biologist. The likelihood of finding anything of significance here, on the other hand, is roughly jack shit. Bridget is temperamentally unsuited to fieldwork, and all that keeps her focused is the thought of the far-off day when she can send younger students and post-grads out in her place.

Fuck the great outdoors. It's a sentiment she never shares with her colleagues, hardy types who spend months willingly camping out and shitting in latrines dug next to trees and in some cases, God help her, lugging their own shit back to civilization in plastic bags so as not to despoil some pristine vista with human feces, even when covered over with nature's own good dirt.

She passes a gate and follows a gravel drive running to a large, two-story cabin of dovetailed logs sticky with resin. A flagstone path leads to a shaded porch. Rundown cabins are scattered about, relics of a tourist ranch, ceilings collapsed from the weight of decades of winter snows, interiors moldy and faded, but log walls still standing. Bright green wild grass grows tall and uncut around the cabins, though the area surrounding the main house is recently mowed. Bridget raps hard on the wooden frame of the screen door. No answer. She walks around the side of the house where she finds a boy tending a pony next to a small stable. The beast, obese and piebald with lovely black eyes, swats at a tenacious fly with its long, cream-colored tail and regards her with slightly more interest than the boy shows.

"Your mother around anywhere?"

"Dead."

"I spoke to a lady in town last week, Ms. Elder? Is this where she lives?"

"Teaching school."

Barely adolescent and painfully ectomorphic, he can't be more than twelve or thirteen. She wonders why the boy isn't in school himself.

"I'm Bridget. What's your name?"

"Cole."

"Nice pony. What's his name?"

"Mysti. She's a mare."

"Is she about to foal?"

Cole laughs and squints as though trying to figure out whether she's putting him on. "No, Ma'am."

She resists the temptation to suggest that he ease up a bit on the feed. "I just wanted to let Ms. Elder know I was heading for that pond up there. Is that part of her property?"

"Guess so."

"Your Dad not around either?"

"No. What you want to go to the lake for?"

"Looking for frogs."

"What's so interesting about them?"

"You know about mutations, right?"

"Nuh-uh."

"You know about genetics? DNA?"

He steps back behind the pony, starts brushing the other side of its neck. "Dr. Glaspie says there's no such thing as DNA. It's all part of The Big Lie."

Great. Thirty seconds in and she's already scandalized the boy. "Who's this Dr. Glaspie?"

"Our principal at school. He's a vet. What's your faith?"

"Methodist," Bridget says, a bureaucratic fact rather than hard-held faith. Her mother was born a Methodist, so when she moved to Colorado that's what she put down on the form.

He pats the pony's neck. "Lake's down that road. Cross the bridge and follow the dirt road up the side of the foothill. I could show you where it's at, if you want."

"You don't need to do that," she says.

"It's okay, I'm done with Mysti, anyway."

"You have a bike?"

He nods. "But better leave yours here. Won't do you much good up there."

Cole pulls a sweatshirt over his tattered blue shirt and they set out down a branch of the gravel drive. She supposes they'll find nothing, or at best nothing but mutants. People still have a hard time understanding that mutations have become the norm, and she suspects that this lake will contain the usual collection of redundant limbs, albinos, and hermaphrodites.

It's a nice day for a hike, though, sunny but cool. When they cross a wooden bridge over the fast river the boy is still talking religion.

"I haven't declared yet. I've only got five more weeks until I'm seventeen, then I've just got a year." He straightens himself up to his full height and deepens his voice, if only slightly. "I'm about halfway decided between the Lutherans and the Assembly of God. Maybe I should give the Methodists a shot, too."

"Sure." She glances at him in search of some sign that he's really pushing seventeen. She wonders if it's something glandular.

"What do they believe, anyway? I mean, besides the usual?"

"Just the usual." Her cheeks warm and she imagines Dr. Pressler watching this exchange: *never, ever discuss religion in the field if you can avoid it.*

"How old are you?"

"Twenty-six."

"Know anything about livestock?"

"Not much. My specialty's herpetology. Reptiles and amphibians."

"There's lizards here still," he says. "No snakes anymore, though."

They walk another mile or so up a foothill road with ruts long overgrown with bright green grasses. The rushing sound of the river dominates until they get to the top of the foothill where a plateau stretches out for a half mile or so before the land climbs again toward the peaks, pale blue and still covered with snow well below the timberline. The sound of the river's current is faint here, the only other sounds the occasional breeze or the whirring of a winged insect. The breeze ruffles a groundcover of sage and grasses, with the occasional yellow or lavender blossom to prove that even at this altitude pollinators still sporadically flit.

The lake turns out to be a small, almost perfectly oval pond. Bridget approaches it with very little hope or interest. Then among the reeds and cattails that line the shallows she spots myriad bobbing clutches of fertilized frog eggs, communally laid in what must amount to the tens of thousands, and she involuntarily holds her breath for a good five seconds. And it gets better: just beyond the egg clutches swims as thriving a larval population as she's ever seen in the wild.

"Got all the polliwogs you can use up here," the boy says, and she nods without looking at him. A few minutes of careful observation follow, the boy maintaining a respectful silence and distance as she dictates and records. Her voice strains as she registers her preliminary report. "The incidence of obvious hermaphrodism among the larvae is extremely low"—here her voice cracks—"and I see only five out of maybe a thousand within a three-meter stretch of bank with evidence of extra limbs." She dips one ungloved hand into the water and teases apart a clutch of soft sticky eggs, eyeing the larvae with an almost lascivious glee.

A walk around the perimeter of the pond, followed by the now somewhat cowed boy, confirms that these conditions persist all the way around the shore, but if the adult frogs who laid the eggs are alive, they're nowhere in evidence.

And then from a few meters ahead comes a loud, plosive splash, unmistakably that of a good-sized adult frog hopping in. Dropping to a crouch she extracts camera from rucksack and begins to record, taking a second to locate the source of the splash through the finder. There, returning to shore with a squirming polliwog halfway into its mouth and down its throat, is the largest, most splendid specimen of American Bullfrog she has ever seen, the greenest and longest legged, his tympanae showing bright and yellow at the sides of his head. As her lens captures the disappearance of the doomed, squirming polliwog down his gullet, Bridget lets out a long, appreciative and unscientific sigh. At the sound, she could swear that the bullfrog turns to look straight at her before taking a short hop into the shallows, returning a moment later with another tadpole's tail wiggling frantically in his enormous maw.

"That's something you'd never catch me doing," the boy says. "Swallowing a live tadpole is what I mean."

Having filmed the frog's predations for five or six minutes, Bridget begins to feel lightheaded, and she becomes conscious of her pulse. Her wrist monitor reads a hundred and six; athletic by nature and necessity, her resting rate hovers typically between forty-five and sixty. She begins to have trouble balancing. Without taking her eye from the viewfinder, Bridget reaches into the pack and takes out an energy bar. With one hand, still tacky from the egg samples, she shreds the top of the wrapper and sticks the bar into the side of her mouth.

"Think I could have one?" the boy says, and she tosses him a bar without looking.

The frog finishes eating and makes his exit via a spectacular leap into the middle of the pond. Bridget turns off the camera, stands, and considers returning down to strike camp immediately to reset it up here; without question, this pond is where she'll spend the rest of the season.

They set off down the road toward the house. Exhausted and exhilarated, she only half registers the boy's monologue, vaguely discerns that his concerns are religion and—more understandably—his upcoming military eligibility, and the notion that marrying a particular local girl might give him an advantage in his choice of Armed Service branches. He's also quite concerned about the welfare of the Hero Dogs in New York City and Washington, D.C. When she turns toward him and puts her hand on his upper arm he freezes like a nocturnal raccoon paralyzed by a flashlight beam.

"Tell Ms. Elder when she gets home that I'd like to set up camp there for the summer."

"Okay."

This request quiets Cole down for the rest of the walk and allows Bridget to rough out a quick proposal in her mind to alter the focus of her summer fieldwork. By the time they reach her bicycle the proposal is done, nothing left but to tap it in and send it.

2.

BRETT MCCAUGHEY, APPROACHING HIS ELEVENTH DECADE with a soul patch three feet long and braided into a stiff triple strand that waggles over the barber's sheet like a rat's tail, has his normally tangled salt-and-pepper hair wet-dark and combed back straight for the scissors. "Saw a hippie chick today," he tells the barber.

"No such thing anymore, Brett."

"You know what I mean, Lamar, kind of a freewheeling young thing with a nice round ass. Juan says she's some kind of government worker here to make sure we're not killing any more bees." He clears his throat, a sound like barnacles being scraped off of a steel hull. "Hell. You even seen any bees since that one Mike Dewey popped?"

"A few around the garden. You know I never used to kill bees because of the honey, but lately every time I see one of the little fuckers it tries to sting me." He snips off a curled end at Brett's collar, with more black strands than gray. "Your Dad keep his hair all his life?"

"Sure did. Course you have to take into account he was all of twenty-three when he bought it."

"Didn't know that."

"Yeah, Korean War. I was a baby then, never knew him."

"This is a real nice head of hair for a man your age."

"So you've told me. I got my original teeth, too."

"Mine are all new."

"That's 'cause your generation ate too much goddamned corn sugar. In my day they made sodas out of cane sugar."

Dr. Edwin Glaspie stops on the sidewalk and opens the door. "You're a week ahead of schedule," Lamar says. Glaspie insists on trimming his thin, white, monkish fringe every two weeks, even though Lamar tells him it's too often.

"Just stopping in to say hello. Happened to notice Brett's bicycle outside. Afternoon, Brett," he says. He's a decade McCaughey's junior but to Lamar Doctor Glaspie has always seemed older, with his slumping posture and shiny pink head. "Been missing you in church lately. Wondering why."

"Oh, I know why, doc." McCaughey lifts a veiny claw from beneath the sheet. "It's 'cause I quit going."

"Any reason I should know about? Anything wrong?"

"I just decided I'd start sleeping in Sundays."

Glaspie sits down. "You know, all your years of churchgoing, I'd hate to see that go out the window."

"I just went because of Claudine making me, and now she's dead I don't have to anymore."

"You want to see Claudine again someday, don't you?"

"You're talking to me like a child, Doc, which is one of those things about you that pisses me off."

Glaspie leans forward and his face brightens as if something wonderful has just occurred to him, hands in front of him, palms out. "I for one believe that we will be reunited with those we love after death."

"Yeah, I know you do, but it seems like a damned dicey proposition to me." And then McCaughey grins, showing off those teeth, yellowed and jagged but definitely his originals. "And you know what? I know I'm going to heaven 'cause I've already been to Vietnam."

Glaspie rises, puts his hand to his forehead and spins a full, tormented 360 degrees before regaining enough composure to speak. "Theologically, that's completely indefensible."

"Guess what? I don't give a shit."

"Doctor Glaspie," Lamar says. "You're agitating my customer, and if he doesn't quit moving his head I'm never going to finish."

"He should be agitated, given what's at stake."

"Out," Lamar says.

Glaspie's mouth hangs open for a couple of beats as he digests the command. "Are you throwing me out?"

"Hell yeah, he's throwing you out," McCaughey says. "Now get going or I'll get up out this chair and fuck you up good."

Glaspie looks at him, eyes glistening, and for a moment Lamar feels sorry for him. The old man sets great store by the respect he commands in town, and there's no pleasure in seeing him taken down a few pegs. "Go now. You can finish the debate later."

Glaspie nods and turns for the door without speaking.

Once he's gone, Brett McCaughey laughs. "Shit. I hate to break it to him but Claudine's nowhere near heaven. If there's a hell, she's roasting in it."

"So, Brett, what's this about Vietnam? I thought you were a draft dodger."

The old man straightens up, turns around to face Lamar. "I was no fucking draft dodger," he yells, spittle flying. "You better apologize."

"Sorry, sorry. I thought that was what you told me. Didn't you spend some time in Sweden?"

"I deserted, Lamar. Big difference. Man, I got drafted and did two thirds of a tour before I blew. I had this girlfriend in Stockholm, name of Maj, good God you should have seen her. Airline stewardess. Goddamn."

"You came back without her?"

"Aw, it was years before I got to come back, she and I'd split long before that. My brother got things fixed for me. He worked for the Lieutenant Governor of Pennsylvania, greased a few palms, got my charges dropped."

"Nice to know some things never change."

"Yeah. It's a great system." He quiets down for a minute or two before piping up again. "You ought to quit shooting your mouth off, Lamar."

"What good's a barber without opinions?"

"I'm not joking. You got a wife and kids. Remember what happened to that hairdresser last year."

"He got disappeared for being queer, not for opening his big mouth. Far as I know, Ivan never had a political thought in his life."

"You just mind your ps and qs. You could be up before a military court and then all bets are off."

A woman in her twenties, idiosyncratically pretty with shoulder length, dark brown hair stops, unlocks her bicycle in front of the shop, and hops on.

"Guess that's your hippie chick."

McCaughey stares, enraptured, as she begins to pedal away, and doesn't speak.

"Not hard to look at," Lamar says, and the old man nods without a word.

Buddy Gallego steps inside and takes a seat, his haircut barely a week old. Lamar suppresses a groan at the sight of him, knowing it's about something he doesn't want to discuss.

"Looky there, it's the mayor," McCaughey says. To Lamar's delight, the two of them immediately start arguing about a tax assessment on McCaughey's bike business, and he lets his mind wander.

He's thinking mostly about tonight's dinner, rabbit stew, and tomorrow's, leg of mutton. Mutton is a biannual treat at best, and the one meal he savors over all others. Tonight after shuttering the shop he'll ride out to Rex Daggett's spring camp and negotiate a price for the meat while styling and trimming his hair and beard, a tradition of long standing between them.

When the old man rises onto his creaking legs to settle up Buddy makes no show of leaving along with him, and when he's out the door Buddy doesn't speak. This silence gives Lamar the fantods, and to counter these he doesn't speak either, just sits down in the barber chair with his arms folded, his face as expressionless as it's possible to get it without local anesthetic, eyes straight on Buddy's.

Buddy breaks first. "Jesus, Lamar, quit it with the evil eye, would you?"

"What's the story, then, Buddy?"

"Why does there have to be a story? Maybe I just feel like hanging out in the barber shop."

Lamar's basilisk stare continues, and he makes a point of focusing his eyes on a point several feet behind Buddy's head.

"Okay. Main event is I got people asking me about you."

"What people?"

"Government people, Lamar."

"Denver-type government people?"

"Higher up."

Though scary, this isn't news. "Asking about what, exactly?"

"Stuff you've been yakking about in some kind of forum, something about the war effort, I don't know exactly what because I don't have time to waste looking at that kind of shit."

"Everything I've said up there is strictly legal, Buddy."

"Probably is, strictly speaking. Thing is, it just isn't good to draw these peoples' attention." He's leaning forward, head jutted forward and index finger thrusting into the empty air.

"There are lots of people on those forums."

Buddy sits back again and lets out a deep breath like a slowly deflating balloon. "This isn't the first time your name's come up. You're a fucking troublemaker."

"They think I'm a troublemaker now? They should have seen me twenty years ago, after I got back from Bhutan."

"They did, Lamar, that's why they're taking you seriously now. Old married man and small town barber, they don't care about that so much. They look at you and they see a radicalized vet. And a black one besides."

"I'm not running for mayor, Buddy."

"What?"

"I'm not running for mayor, if that's what you're really worried about. I know the rumor's been floating around."

"I don't give a shit. The more the merrier."

"Because I thought maybe you were a little worried about it."

He waves Lamar off, shifts his weight to the front and again to the back of the chair. "You know what I always say, an election's nothing but a formality."

For the first time ever Lamar finds Buddy's constant refrain funny rather than offensive. "So you say. Watch it, Buddy, I might change my mind."

"Just watch it, okay? Tone down the rhetoric. It's all right to bitch about the state of the world as long as you're not criticizing the powers that be."

After work, Lamar's on his bicycle, pedaling hard on his way out of town, past the ruins of the old Mobil minimart with its disintegrating gas pumps and the shell of the Radisson, where the ketamine freaks used to squat after the ranks of the methheads thinned out. The ketamine kids got their turn at the disappearing game eventually, and it's been a long time since there was anyone left in Gower who might be tempted to squat.

The Radisson's ghost is the last big hotel standing. The downtown ones were all demolished when it became clear that no one was ever going to come back and ski. Big empty unusable buildings in the center of town were deemed impediments to Gower's imminent resurrection—as what was never quite clear—and Buddy had them razed to their foundations, with generous kickbacks from a Durango-based demolition outfit.

Another seven miles down the road he turns off onto an old forest road and rides uphill until he reaches a fork, where he stops and locks the bike to a tree, out of sight of the road, though no one ever comes here anymore except for the Daggetts.

He hikes another three miles until he comes to Rex's campsite, where the big man sits crosslegged before a fire.

"Rex. You got my mutton?"

"Got it right here." Rex indicates a sealed foil bag and stands, switches on a couple of incandescent towers that provide a startling illumination, bright enough for a proper haircut, and sits down in his canvas folding chair.

"What are we doing tonight?" Since this is only a twice-yearly ritual it seems worth asking, though the answer is always the same.

"As usual." Rex settles back into the chair and closes his eyes. "Wait a minute, though—I had a good idea for my braid."

An hour and a half later Lamar's hiking back down in the dark, the cold sack of mutton on his back, looking forward to tomorrow and half wondering if he shouldn't run for Buddy's seat after all. He could make a decent showing, he knows that, even if Buddy's right about it being a rubber stamp. Maybe he could show it up as the rigged game it's always been. For a moment he allows the notion to excite him, then he catches himself and laughs at the naïveté of it. Buddy's right; nobody gives a good goddamn how he got into office as long as he keeps the checks coming in from the mining company, keeps subsidizing their solar gear, keeps telling them how much better off they are than those supposedly more prosperous towns that are on the Big Grid. Cleanest water in North America. A TarMart truck in every two months as long as the roads are passable. Decent makework for released Armed Service personnel, particularly the infirm.

He wants to get home and cook up tonight's meal and wait for the girls to go to bed so he can get onto the forum, but Buddy's warning makes him nervous. Just because bitching in public isn't illegal doesn't mean it can't get him into trouble, and he decides to put a lid on it for a while, maybe figure out how people manage to do it anonymously. Still it rankles, and before he knows it he's stomping again, double-timing it to the fork in the road where his bicycle waits.

But it's not there. He wonders if he's looking at the wrong tree until he sees the chain, sliced through, looped around the base of the spruce. The chain is titanium and the cut is clean, and he starts backing into the woods as quietly as he can.

"Mr. Collins? Could you step out of there, please?" The voice is soft and polite, which scares him more than a growl or gunshot.

"Who's that?"

As soon as he opens his mouth the fork in the road is illuminated by half a dozen floods, and as many men step out of the trees, dressed in flak jackets and holding automatic weapons.

"We'd like to have a word with you."

He can feel his jaw going slack, and his joints don't feel right, his knees almost unable to keep him upright. He doesn't think he could run at all, much less outrun these guys, one of whom, he now sees, is holding his bicycle.

"We've got a vehicle waiting down the hill."

He steps forward, wanting to cry but unable to summon any outward show of emotion. He thinks of the girls and, despite himself, of the mutton, wishes they would have come for him two days later, but of course this trip into the boonies was too tempting an opportunity for them to pass up. And then he thinks of Rex, armed like a commando and hating the government like any good mountain man. He wouldn't hesitate to pin these security contractors down and pick them off one by one, would do it gladly for his old friend and barber. He fills his lungs with the cool, thin piney air of the glade and expels it with all his strength. "Rex! Help!"

But he understands that Rex is too far away to hear him, and he receives the hot shock to the back of his neck with something like equanimity. Lamar goes down to the soft carpet of pine needles, a few of them gently pricking his cheek and hands, and anticipating the next blow he thinks he should have kept his opinions to himself after all.

3

IN HER DREAM Darla is twelve years old, lying on the living room carpet in front of the TV with her chin cupped in her hands, watching the Beatles on Ed Sullivan with her parents, her Dad spewing invective at the screen from his La-Z-Boy while her mother frets silently on the davenport. She snaps awake in the dark and marvels at the accuracy of the dream's detail, right down to the weave on the upholstery and the shag of the carpet and the fact that Ed Sullivan used to be on Channel 4.

She's on the street before sunrise in an old cheerleader's uniform she found long ago among the abandoned costume racks in the Opera House basement. The colors are wrong, black and gold—what the fuck kind of school is that, anyway? Blue and red is what you want, baby, blue and red—with a demented kind of Frankensteiny mascot chomping on a stalk of wheat. Damn, though, she sure fills it out nice, stopping in front of the grocery store as the first light turns the sky the color of a peach and admiring her fine self in the window, that old Fleetwood Mac song about drowning a gypsy in the sea of love ricocheting off the old synapses and setting off the still-irresistible metronome in her hips. She should open up a strip joint is what she ought to do. Give the people what they want, and what they want is Darla, *baby*.

In front of Consuela's she sits on the stoop wishing it was still open for breakfast, not that she likes breakfast but she'd sure like some coffee or even tea, remember that good herbal shit Tinnie used to drink? Fucking chicory's what she gets, though, unless Juan's in a real generous mood. And not until eleven thirty when he opens up for lunch. *Get a hot plate, Darla, why don't you? Yeah, you'd fuckin' love that you greaser piece of shit, you'd never have to put up with my shit again, would you? Guess what motherfucker, no such luck.*

The conversation goes on until she tires of taking both her and Juan's parts and she stands up. There's the familiar smell of something dead in the air, something pretty good-sized, she thinks. She's been smelling it for a few days now, off and on, little molecules of decomposing mammal exciting her olfactory nerve. It occurs to her that it could be something endangered, maybe. Find the carcass and sell it to the Museum of Natural History in Denver, if it's there anymore.

On her way to find the stink she stops in front of the school, that's always good in the morning. She likes watching the kids arrive, books under their arms or crossed in front of their chests, likes how fucking cheerful they all are, how they don't seem to give a shit yet.

I believe that children are from the future, as Whitney sang so beautifully. So fucking true. And there's old Ed Glaspie, watching them like a goddamn shepherd. She considers doing a cheer or two from the old repertoire, maybe ending with a split, just to fuck with him. She tries to remember whether or not she's wearing panties; lifting the pleats of the short gold skirt she finds to her delight that she is, clean ones, too. Something in Glaspie's face stops her though, a look of grandfatherly affection toward his flock, and she moves on in search of the source of the cadaver smell.

Walking toward her is that fucking social worker with that solicitous look on her face like she's about to start asking apparently innocuous questions that are in fact designed to make Darla seem like a crazy old lady so they can evict her from the Opera House and send her over to Boulder for experiments, which everybody with half a brain knows is the whole reason the county still has social workers.

"Two can play at that game, whoretoilet," she says before the social worker gets a word out.

She's startled. Good. Get the upper hand right the fuck away, never let it go.

"Beg your pardon, Darla?"

"You heard me, munch."

The social worker tilts her head sideways and looks like she's never been treated to that particular epithet before. If Darla was a dyke she wouldn't do this gal for anything—that Dippity-Do flip is straight out of 1967—but that galpal of hers, the carpenter, she's another matter entirely.

Carpenter-muncher, she thinks. Or did she just say it? Probably the former, since the social worker is still smiling.

"You have a good day, Darla."

"Fuckin' A right, I'm fixing to have a hell of a day. Gonna find me a dead animal and sell it to the Museum of Natural motherfuckin' History. I'm on the trail right now."

The woman waggles her caboose in the direction of the school in an unseemly hurry. Darla raises her nose into the wind and takes a deep whiff. Subtle traces of the carcass's odor linger, but it's weak, that weird dead animal smell that starts to have a kind of sweet overtone, like a beehive after the honey's gone. She's clearly headed the wrong way.

If I were a decomposing animal, where would I be?

She's thinking of a time at her grandmother's house in Missouri when a big old opossum died underneath a bush and gave off a smell just like this one, though not as strong. One of her uncles came over and got it out with a shovel and threw the fucker in the trash while her grandma stood there supervising the job. How come there aren't any old ladies like that anymore, with their hair all gray and piled up on their heads and smelling like powder?

She passes uphill through town and the scent intensifies until near Eighth where nobody lives or even goes. The smell packs a real wallop.

Outside a little house, abandoned for years even by the squatters who lived here last, she finds the source of the stink, curled up on the busted up concrete. Rex Daggett is sitting there on the curb, looking like he's giving some serious thought to cutting the thing up and making off with it. Fine with her, this isn't museum-quality material anyway, and she's pretty sure the museum must already have a few elk in the collection.

"What you figure happened to her?" she asks Rex.

He squints. "Looks to me like she was trying to drop a calf and just gave up on it."

"I been smelling her a couple days now. Thought it might be something valuable."

"Time you smelled her she was past eating. Dogs and crows been doing a pretty good job chowing down on her anyway."

"Too bad. She's good-sized."

"That she is. You needing any meat?"

"Nothing big. I could use some rabbits for the freezer, though. Pay you later."

"The hell you will. When your daughter the mayor got my Dad out of that killing scrape with the state, that paid for you and your family's meat for life. The Daggetts don't forget."

Which is funny because Darla had indeed forgotten about that whole business. Shit, it's decades since her daughter even lived here.

Rex stands up, holds his bad knee and winces. "You take care, Darla."

He limps off up into the trees and Darla squints into the window of an abandoned house she remembers from the old days, with a living room full of debris from when the squatters had pretty much taken over this town. How long have they been gone now? You could turn all these little cottages into ski chalets if you wanted. All we'd need would be a little less snow come wintertime and we'd be back the fuck in business.

She heads back in the direction of home, trying to figure out how to make it happen.

4

STACEY ELDER SHOWS BRIDGET INTO A LIVING ROOM CHAIR, brings her a cup of powdered chicory and sits leaning forward, chin on her hands.

"So it's as good as I said, right?" Stacey says.

Bridget swigs a mouthful of the wretched, thin chicory. "I'd be up there all through the spring and summer and probably part of the fall, too."

"Fine with me. You want some more chicory?"

"No, I'm all right." This easy acquiescence gives her pause. "I assume this will be okay with your husband, then?"

Stacey's face goes perfectly blank for a moment, then her smile returns. "My husband doesn't have any say over it for the time being." Then she sits back, holding her hands over her crossed knees, lips pressed tightly together.

Bridget can't help pursuing it, mostly out of a fear that the husband will turn out to have a different opinion. "Does he work in town, or on the property here?"

"My husband is rumored to be in the Armed Services, but I have no idea when or if to expect his return. In any case the land is mine, not his."

Stacey's formal tone suggests she's not looking for pity, so Bridget just nods. "I'd better get up there and pitch camp." She sips the last of her chicory.

"It's getting late for that. Why don't you spend the night in the guest room tonight and eat dinner here, and you can get an early start in the morning?"

Another reminder of the property's dude ranch origins is the still opulent guest bedroom, finished with cedar, with its own bathroom with running water and a toilet. Bridget flops down on the big bed, her first in six weeks, and closes her eyes.

When Stacey's knock comes at the door the sun is nearly down and the room considerably darker, and with some difficulty she orients herself, still feeling alarmed from a dream of rotting, broken teeth. She struggles to rid herself of the lingering impression of spitting out chunks of bloody, pulpy enamel onto a shattered concrete sidewalk as she wept.

Over dinner Stacey dominates the conversation with talk of politics and books, neither of which are particular interests of Bridget's. They drink weak beer from bottles rewashed so many times they're more gray than brown, and though Cole is allowed one he takes only a few tiny sips. He has on an ancient t-shirt bearing the faded and scuffed image of a murdered rock star, dead six decades now. The neck and sleeves are in tatters and the seams largely split.

"Nice shirt," Bridget says.

Cole blushes and Stacey rolls her eyes. "I tried to get him to take it off. It's his Dad's. I ought to use it for dusting."

"It's my favorite shirt," Cole says.

"I don't remember you ever wearing it before. Anyway what do you care about this guy? Jesus, he was dead before I was born, even." Stacey folds her hands together alongside her cheek, elbows on the table. "So are you working on your doctorate, or is this strictly work for the state?"

"I'm post-doc. University has a contract with the State Department of Biological Affairs. I'll publish something, eventually."

"I thought the frogs were supposed to be doing better."

"Not anymore. They're dying off most places around here, too. I hardly found any at my first camp."

"Maybe it was the wrong altitude. Too low."

"It's higher up where you wouldn't expect to see them," Bridget says. "That's what's so weird about your pond. No one's seen any frogs at this altitude in Colorado in twenty years, probably."

"We have," Cole says.

"There aren't any fish in that pond, are there?"

"Lake," Stacey says. "They used to stock it thirty, forty years ago, for little kids and for people who didn't want to wade in the river. When I was a little girl we'd swim in it, as long as nobody was fishing."

"You grew up here?"

"I did. Went away to college in Los Angeles, back in the days when that was easy to do. My God, every single person I knew out there had a car. Literally every single adult."

Bridget fights not to roll her eyes. "That's interesting."

"And you wouldn't think anything of driving twenty, thirty miles running errands. And you'd have a radio in your car so you could listen to the news or music and not go out of your mind from boredom."

And the sidewalks were paved with spongecake, and shit smelled like flowers, and the orgasms were amazing, better than the crappy ones you kids have to settle for these days. "Yeah, my Mom always talks about that."

"Anyway, UCLA, class of '18. I was an Art History major, which even thirty years ago seemed kind of pointless, but if I'd had any idea... When I came back here I was thirty, divorced, defaulted on a mortgage, credit ruined, couple of little kids to raise. So I got married again."

"To Cole's Dad," Bridget says, less out of actual interest than to prove she's paying attention.

"He was after. This time it was to Buddy Gallego. We split up when my kids were teenagers. My daughter's a carpenter, has a little girl, son's a notary, which is the closest thing we have to a lawyer. All we need, anyway. Buddy's the mayor now."

Bridget nods, in the middle of a swig, but misses her chance to get a word in; by the time she's swallowed Stacey has taken a deep breath and is back on a roll.

"So anyway, I've been teaching all this time, English and

American History and Spanish and Bible as History. When my two graduated I thought I'd leave town again, but I owned this pretty patch of land, which isn't really worth anything these days but I wouldn't want to lose it. And then I was married to Ted Elder. Until he up and blew town." A wistful expression flits across her face.

"He joined the Armed Services," Cole says.

Stacey speaks very carefully, with an eye on the boy. "He was either forcibly conscripted or he ran away and joined, we're not sure."

"I got a mail from him a month after he left, said everything was a-okay and all systems go," Cole says, seated now with his thin arms folded across his chest, glaring at his apostate stepmother.

"All I know is I never heard from him directly, just from the Armed Services Special Technical Contracting Department, and I wasn't able to trace the message to its source."

"In the Armed Services they don't let you say where you are. That's the rules."

"Fine. Anyway, he's never once contacted me, his wife, who's got custody of his minor son, which seems really I consider very strange. Especially for a fast guy with a genius IQ and upper degrees in chemistry, engineering, and electronics. Hard to imagine him not finding a way to get around the Armed Services regs." Stacey slugs down the remains of her third beer and opens a fourth. "So where're you from?"

"Kansas."

"Flatlander, huh? Grew up dreaming about the mountains and the streams? Couldn't wait to get away?"

"I ended up in Boulder because of a scholarship. I've never really cared much about the mountains one way or the other."

"Good for you, I hate all that John Denver shit myself."

Cole perks up visibly at the vulgarity.

"Nothing against the mountains," Bridget says.

"No, I know, but listen, you should have seen Gower twenty, thirty years ago. There used to be tourists here all summer, rich tourists, for the fly fishing, and in the winter to ski. It was never Aspen or Breckenridge, but we had crowds and it was expensive, Jesus Christ, was it expensive. Can you picture that? Coming here in the wintertime now? Voluntarily? It's like fucking Dogpatch around here anymore."

The boy shoots upright in shock at the forbidden word, and gazes dumbfounded at Bridget, as if to confirm that she heard it, too, and straight from the lips of his stepmother, the school-teacher. Stacey soldiers tipsily on, unaware of her own transgression.

"But anyhow, I guess this is where I'll end up buried. Hopefully not sooner rather than later. Later rather than sooner."

Bridget stands and picks up her plate. "Can I help you clean up?"

The late nap keeps Bridget awake, and at two-thirty in the morning she dresses and creeps downstairs, gearbag slung over her shoulder. At the door she puts her boots on and begins the hike up the trail to the pond. The full moon is high and so bright that she doesn't turn on the lamp in her hand, letting the trail before her shine pale blue in the still air. She wishes for the umpteenth time on this trip that she'd brought her telescope along, but long-distance traveling on a bike has its downsides. She sees Jupiter—or is it Saturn?—ten degrees off the moon, and further down the ecliptic will be Mars, if she's out late enough.

When the pond comes into sight she hears no amphibian sounds, no croaking or splashing, just crickets chirping and the sound of her own feet brushing against the long grass. And then she hears it, a loud, distinctive, bellowing cry—the mating call of the American Bullfrog. She waits for another male to join in, and within seconds it comes, followed by another and another until there's a discordant, frantic chorus. She puts the camera to her eye, sets it for night vision, and scans the area of the pond, walking slowly and cautiously. Through the finder she sees a calling male and thinks he may be the same big one she saw earlier. The bull sits on the muddy bank, calling out for love, and for a moment Bridget feels unaccountably sorry for him.

What comes next is sufficiently unexpected that it takes her a moment to recover her wits sufficiently to start the recording: within twenty seconds of the start of the croaking females of all shapes, colors, and sizes are jumping out of the weeds, swimming from further down the shore, even hopping in from the copse of trees bordering the stream that feeds the pond.

This is a larger group of amphibians than she thought existed anywhere in North America. Bridget keeps her finder on the big male; the first female he deigns to mount is even bigger than he is and very pale in color, at least as seen through the camera. His attempt at amplexus is heroic and almost funny; his forelegs barely cover her shoulders, but as she lays a monstrous clutch of eggs he does his duty, deposits the requisite load of semen there-upon, the whole business shining in the moonlight through her lens. Once his frenzied task is accomplished he takes a splendid backward somersault from her back. Abandoned, the big female leaps three feet into the air, hits the water headfirst, and disap-pears under it. Before she's out of sight the bull has mounted her successor, and she lays her clutch atop the previous batch as the male fertilizes them in a frenzy of groping. Bridget pulls back for a shot of the whole breeding ground, stunned at the dimensions of it. Multiple, less dominant males fight for the chance to fertilize eggs that a single female is laying next to a cluster of cattails. They croak and claw at one another in an effort to get close enough to her hindquarters.

This is the first large-scale mating she's ever witnessed, and as far as she knows it may be the only one going on in all of North America tonight. A colony of healthy animals taking advantage of a very brief climatological window to reproduce *en masse* shouldn't be worthy of note, but given the fragile, even moribund state of the amphibian class in the world it comes close to qualifying as miraculous.

This frog orgy is going to make Bridget famous.

5

Mysti whinnies and stomps her front hooves, waiting to be brushed and fed. Half an hour off his weekday schedule, Cole fills her trough and brushes her, thinks what a fine pony she is, and feels ashamed at taking such an animal for granted. She tucks into her oats and corn, and he notes with pleasure the narrowing distance between her belly and the ground. He imagines his Dad would be pleased with her, allows himself to hope that he'll come back in time to see him show her at the County Ag Festival.

A minute later the hope transforms itself into doubt and a grim sense that his father will never come back, that he'll be killed in action. An intrusive, nagging thought follows, as it often does, this pessimistic one, the idea that Stacey's right, that his old man just got tired of the whole town of Gower and hopped a freighter to China. Then he squints as hard as he can, until the backs of his eyelids go from red to an electric purple, and he prays to God for forgiveness.

When he steps into the school office forty-five minutes later Dr. Glaspie looks up from his reading, an ancient paperback novel minus its cover, spine held together with black electrical tape. To Cole's relief, the doctor smiles out the corner of his mouth and starts telling him the plot of the book he's reading, a thriller about the Rapture. "You really ought to start reading these, there's a whole series of them. Good Christian adventure stuff."

"I'm not much on made-up stories, really."

"I'm not either, Cole, and I still can't get enough of these. I read 'em the first time forty-odd years ago when they were new, and I'll bet you I've read 'em fifteen times since. I tell you what, when school's out in September I'll lend you the whole series and you can bring 'em back in June."

Upon entering the Quonset hut where his Bible as History III section meets Cole draws a glare from the teacher, Miss Ingelblad, and snickers from his classmates as he hands her his Late Pass. He purposely takes a chair behind Greta Gallego, whose rear end and long red hair he will pointedly, rigorously avoid staring at throughout the class as a test of will.

Five minutes later he's lost track of Miss Ingelblad's theory on the nature of the whale that swallowed Jonah—she believes it was a giant fish, perhaps an extinct species of tuna, since no known whale has a throat that would permit the ingress of a fully grown man—his thoughts focused instead on a recurrent fantasy of being trapped with Greta in a remote cabin with no fireplace and a single blanket for warmth after snowfall.

The only other boy in his class is taller, smarter, more athletic, and better looking than Cole—so much so that none of the girls has decided so far to aim her sights lower. They'll cut their losses eventually, though; Neal Babb has confessed to Cole that he knows his soulmate to be tiny, blonde Debbie Corcoran, she of the perfect, pouting face and the elephantine ears artfully hidden by those long blonde locks. A year or two from now, after Neal has taken Debbie as his bride, Cole will swoop in and win brokenhearted, vulnerable Greta.

He returns his attention to Miss Ingelblad and finds her still digressing on the potential of various genera of carnivorous fish to swallow a man without chewing him to death. When the timer goes off and the class moves on to Algebra, Miss Ingelblad asks him to stay behind, and he sinks back down into one of the folding chairs.

"How are you getting along with your classmates?"

"Okay, I guess."

"No more problems with Neal?" At the beginning of the year Neal had pinned him down to the floor of the Quonset hut after Cole swung at him for saying that Cole's Dad had run out on him and Stacey, but they'd gotten over it quickly enough.

"Not anymore."

"Is there a reason you sit right behind Greta every day?"

"I don't always."

"Yes, you do. You're always the only one behind the other students, and it's always right behind Greta. From now on there's going to be one row. Understood?"

"Yes, Ma'am."

"I know your Dad's away, Cole. Is there anything you'd like to talk about?"

"No, Ma'am."

"Because I know there are some subjects that guys discuss with their Dads, and it's better you get that kind of information from an adult. If you're not comfortable talking to Stacey then you can talk to me. Or if the fact that I'm a woman bothers you, you could talk to Dr. Glaspie."

His face is hot, and his arms are cold with sweat. For the first time Miss Ingelblad is giving him an erection. Even more horrifying, he finds that his humiliating condition is bringing tears to his eyes.

What in God's name is wrong with him all of a sudden?

This being Wednesday, the school day is over after Algebra and Christian Studies. The way back home is slow and Cole finds himself brooding over what Stacey said at dinner the other night about his Dad. He's ashamed of it, but there are times when he wonders whether his father did just up and leave on purpose. But if it was true, if he'd just run off to sell his fresh-water patents, he'd have come back for Cole, at least, if not Stacey. No, his Dad had been shanghaied into the Armed Services and that was that.

At home he feeds and grooms Mysti, and then locks himself in the guest bathroom. He sometimes thinks he'd like to call down some Sim'n'Stims from overseas the way Neal Babb does, but Stacey would find them on the bill at the end of the month, and anyway the one Neal showed him made him a little bit queasy. Without meaning to he takes a new tack—his usual healthy thoughts of Greta at first interspersed with shameful, quickly dismissed but highly effective ones of Miss Ingelblad—after which he fires up the fully charged screen.

The first signal he captures is that of an agricultural show, a very thin redheaded woman talking in an agitated way about corn rot and the dangers it presents to the war effort. Cole moves quickly on to the next offering, a documentary about the First Lady's work with wounded paramilitary personnel. The narrator oversells her youth and beauty, in Cole's opinion, and again he moves on, this time to a movie about an army deserter robbing a church and holding the parishioners hostage, the deserter played by an actor who in real life quit show business to join an Armed Forces Special Combat Unit and died gloriously in a truck crash. Cole knows immediately how it will end, as he always does.

Despite the ideal time of day and the cloudless sky there's nothing else legible on the band, and he powers the set down, wishing he lived in a city connected to the Big Grid where he could watch whatever he wanted any time of day.

From his wallet he takes a weathered sheet of notebook paper and smoothes it out on the kitchen table.

GOALS FOR THIS YEAR

1. Get Mysti ready Fr County Ag Fest

fifteen minutes grooming morning + Nite

2. Find out where Neal Got Condem At

Dont let him on to why I want to know

```
3. Stay after School + Wrk on Miuscles
4. LEARN MORE BIBLE
Esp New Test.
5. PICK A FAITH ALREADY!!!!!
6. QUIT SELF POLUTION!
(REMEMBER SQUIRLY OLD GUY USED to HANG AROUND
BUS DEEPO!!)
7. START CHINESE!!!
(REMEMBER WHAT DAD SAID!)
```

He takes his pencil to the last goal.

```
8. FIND OUT WHERE DAD IS.
```

With a paper grocery sack filled with an offering of pemmican and taffy, Cole hikes up the foothill road to Chouteau Lake, where he finds Bridget outside her tent taking notes. With headphones covering both ears she still hasn't noticed him, and he lowers himself to his knees and touches his fingertips to her shoulder.

Taking in a sharp breath she flips onto her back and brandishes an electronic device he's seen on television whose function he doesn't precisely understand apart from the fact that it can send a lethal electric charge through a human body. By this time he's jumped back several feet, hands in the air, and counts himself lucky that his pants are still dry.

She lets out the breath and lowers the weapon, pulls off her headphones. Her wavy hair is tangled and on her forehead a few strands are matted with sweat.

"Sorry."

"Shit, you really scared me." To his relief she laughs. Her

mouth is crooked, lower in the middle than at the ends, which curl downward and give her a permanent sardonic expression that makes Cole squirm without understanding why.

He holds out the bag. "Brought you a snack."

Peering into it her face goes from puzzlement to disappointment to cheerful, feigned gratitude. "Deer jerky. Great."

"Pemmican."

"Same thing, right?"

"I don't know." She's wearing a thin gray cotton tank top, dark with sweat at the sternum and beneath the arms, and he wants more than anything in the world to stare at her breasts. "Well, I'll see you later."

"You're leaving already?"

"Aren't you busy?"

"I can take a break."

He can feel his heartbeat way up in his throat. "Okay," he says, and he sits down. "Where do you live in Boulder?" he croaks.

"University housing. Cruddy but cheap."

"Dr. Glaspie and his wife went to Boulder a couple of times. Full of immigrants, I hear. Denver's supposed to be real bad."

"Pretty bad. Not the immigrants' fault, though."

Sensing disapproval he makes a note not to knock immigrants anymore. "You ever go over there? To Denver?"

"Boulder's a Federal district, so we get pretty much everything we need right in town."

He nods, picks a blade of long grass and mashes the pulpy part, then holds it under his nose for a deep whiff. "How do you get to be a biologist?"

"You take it in college, then afterwards graduate school."

"Maybe that's what I'll do. I was thinking about veterinary anyway, that's kind of close."

She nods, takes out a piece of pemmican and smells it, then gnaws off a stringy corner. It's rough chewing and her expression is ambiguous as she works at it, but as the meat softens she seems pleased.

"The Methodist service starts at nine on Sunday morning. I thought maybe I might go with you since I'm thinking about maybe declaring for them."

"Oh." She's surprised, and for just a second she seems like she's about to laugh. She speaks very carefully. "See, Cole, I don't really go to church."

He stares at her with a mixture of envy, admiration, and horror. "You shouldn't say stuff like that."

"In Boulder we're under Federal jurisdiction. You don't have to actually go, as long as you've declared, so lots of people don't."

"Here you pretty much do have to."

"Well, I'm transient, and I'm still registered as a resident of Boulder, so unless they want to come up here and make an issue of it I won't be going. And I'll have work to do. It's supposed to get up to about eighty Sunday."

"Eighty's warm for springtime."

"For here, maybe. Hold on a sec..." She calls up some data on her screen. "It's a hundred and nine degrees in Chicago today, ninety-nine in Los Angeles, a hundred and twelve in New York."

"You been to any of those places?"

"Two years ago. Conference at the Museum of Natural History

in New York."

"Was it real crowded and smelly?"

"I was at the museum pretty much the whole time."

"How'd you get there?"

"Flew."

Can she really be as jaded as she sounds? Cole has to struggle to keep his jaw from going slack and his eyebrows from shooting scalpward. "What's it like on an airplane?"

"Noisy. And I was in Upright Class, which was pretty uncomfortable."

"Did you really feel the ground moving away from you when it took off?"

"Yeah, actually I did."

He moves to leave. "See you soon. I might come up again in a day or two."

"Maybe sometime you can ride that pony of yours up here."

Cole starts laughing, and it takes him a moment to take notice of the puzzled look in Bridget's eyes. "Can't ride Mysti," he says.

"Really?"

He laughs again, can't help it, at the thought of riding Mysti. He'd barely be able to straddle her.

A couple of days later he tells the story to Dr. Glaspie, who gets a good chortle out of it too. It's a quiet moment in the vet's surgery, in the midst of a discussion of Mysti's prospects.

"Next week I'll bring the scale out in the county van and we'll weigh her. Eyeballing her the other day, though, I'd say she'd beat any of last year's by a hundred pounds."

"It's the corn added to the oats."

"That could well be part of it, but what I see is an animal responding to devoted care. You're doing a fine job, boy."

"Thanks."

Looking at Cole, Dr. Glaspie wrinkles his forehead and raises one bushy white eyebrow. "Miss Ingelblad told me you might have some questions about things."

"No, sir."

This seems to relieve Dr. Glaspie, who exhales deeply, his posture slumping. "You hear from your Dad since that last time?"

"No, sir."

"I wouldn't worry about it. You know they're not allowed to write home the way they used to, just too much trouble for the Armed Services making sure they don't give away any secrets like where they're fighting at. It sure was different when my boys were in the services."

"I guess so."

"They used to be able to call home on a cell phone whenever they pleased. Even in the middle of winter they could talk to their mother from halfway around the world, from Pyongyang or Jakarta or what have you."

"That sounds pretty good."

"It was a wickeder world, though. My gosh, the things a boy your age might have come across, just watching the television. All sorts of crazy ideas."

Cole scratches his upper lip. "Dr. Glaspie, what do you think happened to Lamar really?"

"Who can say? He's not here to tell us."

"You think the government took him away?"

"Foolishness. For all we know it may have been a gang of foreign terrorists."

Cole's eyelids lock in their widest position. "In Gower?"

The doctor stares at the ceiling for a minute, revealing a patch of beard under his chin, as if his razor missed the same spot three or four days running. Then he snaps his head abruptly back down, and Cole is embarrassed to be caught looking.

"Say, I got something sent this week, and I printed it up for you." The Doctor hands him a sheaf of shiny printouts. "They send this out to all the vets in the Hero Dog Support Network. Thought you might like a look."

Cole leafs through sections, each illustrated with spectacular photos, on all the branches of the Hero Dog Service: Fire, Police, Lifeguard, Disease Sniffers, and Corpse Rescue. He's discomfited at the amount of space dedicated to the last group; he understands that they're an essential part of the National Security Effort, but he finds their work repulsive and wishes they could be relegated to some other, less exalted category.

"Do you know if there's any way to find out which branch you're going to be supporting?"

The doctor shakes his head. "I don't think so."

"What if you want to support one particular group? Like the Fire Dogs?"

"Tell you what, why don't you give a little more thought to your schoolwork and let the experts in Washington decide which kind of dogs get your support?"

"I guess that's all right," Cole says, but he makes a silent vow to do everything he can to make sure it's one of the other branches.

Somebody else can help out with Corpse Rescue.

6

ON BRIDGET'S THIRD AFTERNOON IN THE NEW CAMP she follows the path of the stream for five miles up the mountain and finds nothing significant. She'll have to go further at some point, but the project has been so fruitful thus far that she feels free to laze away the end of one afternoon. She's a dozen or so meters from the tent when the man steps out from the copse of aspen and calls to her in a voice loud and deep, hoarse and slurry. His cry is unintelligible but carries an unmistakably confrontational note, and reaching into the front pocket of her coveralls for the grizzly zapper she wishes she had a gun instead.

His beard, thick and blond, is bracketed by a pair of Brunhilde-ish golden braids plaited together under it, giving him the air of a transgendered Viking. He speaks again. "I got something to show you, lady."

Her grip on the taser tightens as he opens a bag and pulls out, by one delicate, outstretched wing, a dead hummingbird. "What you think of that?"

"Where'd you find it?" she asks. Post-Bakker cladistic reshufflings notwithstanding, birds are outside her realm. This one is lovely, though, the only one she's ever seen with its wings neither beating invisibly nor folded against its sides. The inside of the wing is a shiny white with tinges of iridescent gray toward the torso, almost sparkling, and the head with its delicate hypodermic beak dangles limp.

"I didn't find it, I shot the little fucker."

"Shot it? Really?" This does pique her interest, because she can't imagine how even a good shot could hit such a tiny, quick-flitting thing, or with what weapon.

"Shot it with a pellet and there ain't shit you can do about it."

She makes a mighty effort to keep her voice and features calm. "Why would I want to do anything about it?"

"You're the state biologist, ain't you?"

"I'm only interested in the frogs. Anyway, I'm no enforcement agent."

"Bullshit. Last year Mike Dewey got a three-hundred dollar fine for killing a goddamn honeybee."

"What'd he kill it for?"

"Dumb son of a bitch was trying to prove something right in front of Donny Waxman."

"Who's he?"

"Chief of Police in Gower. Anyway the damn bees are worse than they ever were. My brother Lon got stung right on the nose last year before it started getting cold."

"Uh-huh."

"So why the fuck can't we kill 'em?"

"You can, as far as I'm concerned. Not much I can do if you want to poison a whole hive."

He relaxes, and minus its surly menace his big, square face takes on a not altogether unpalatable warmth. "I guess that's all right, then. Just rankles the shit out of me, though, got all kinds of shit going on with deer and shit dying off and they won't do fucky fuck about that, but catch a man stomping on a bumblebee.... So what's the deal with the frogs anyway?"

"Just cataloging, trying to figure out why some strains survive and some don't."

He converts quickly from potential assassin to would-be assistant, going off on a litany of mutant amphibia he's seen—or, she strongly suspects, imagined—in the last fifteen or so years, the most fanciful examples being a conjoined male-female twin fertilizing its own eggs and a footlong bullfrog with eight eyes. He points a finger the size of a hot dog in the direction she's just come from. "Up there at a little pond below the peak, five, six years ago, there was a whole bunch of weird shit up there for a while. Guess it's mostly gone now." He looks in that direction for a minute. "Sorry I come down kind of half-cocked on you. Anybody gives you any shit up here, Stacey Elder knows where to get me. Name's Rex Daggett, and me and my boys'll back you up good."

At dinnertime the sky is mostly clear, the remaining clouds puffy and rose-colored, the air smelling exceptionally clean. It's six-thirty when Bridget passes the house, and she stops to knock.

"Got a whole bunch of meal vouchers I haven't used yet. I was thinking I'd take you out to dinner."

Flustered, Stacey steps outside and closes the door. "Actually, I'm meeting someone for dinner in town. Usually Cole has Bible Study with the Assembly of God Tuesdays but he says he's not going anymore. It'd be a real lifesaver if you could invite him along with you."

Inside she sees Cole sitting at a table working on a lesson, wonders why he can't be left at home alone at his age. She shrugs; beats eating alone. "Sure, we'll talk frogs and horses."

She opens the door and sticks her head inside. "Hey, Cole, how'd you like to have dinner in town with Bridget?"

He snaps to attention, nods without a word, his eyes wide in a way that makes his aspect even more childish than usual, and knocks his chair into the table reaching for his windbreaker.

"Hi," he says to Bridget on the porch, "Wait just a sec while I feed Mysti." He runs around the corner, boots stomping on the wood porch until he vaults the rail.

Stacey leans against the doorsill, eyes closed, hands to her temples. "Thanks a million. He really doesn't like me much, but when we're in town he's on me like white on rice."

His footfalls can be heard across the gravel, followed by the sound of his bike being taken off the side of the house. Stacey lowers her voice. "Would've been awkward if you hadn't shown up."

Consuela's vaguely Mexican cuisine is supplemented with fried trout, rabbitburgers and cold sandwiches. Though the county is officially dry it nonetheless serves the State Beverage of Colorado, thanks to the owner's relationship by marriage to the mayor, whose photograph hangs on the wall above the grill, alternately smiling and winking, depending upon the viewer's angle.

"A girl in my class has eleven toes," Cole says. "Dr. Glaspie was going to cut the extra off but they wouldn't let him and now she walks crooked."

"Oh."

"My Dad can make salt water into plain. He figured it out while he was working for the mayor."

"Hmm. Lot of people would like to know how to do that."

"I'm not kidding. He can. Probably that's why the Armed Services wanted him so bad."

The owner stops by and introduces himself as Juan Stevens, the grandson of Consuela herself, self-consciously brushing his fingertips over close-cropped gray hair. He offers her a second beer on the house, then snaps his fingers at the lone waitress, a haggard woman in an ancient polyester uniform.

"Another Coors, Sal." Juan cocks his thumb in her direction. "Dumb as a bag of hammers. Got a husband won't work since he fell off a scaffold drunk. Says he's got headaches." He makes a sad face and mimes brushing away a tear.

As Sal approaches the table Bridget winces when Juan slaps her on the ass, eliciting a laugh. "Best watch it, Juan, I'll go down to the notary's and file a claim on you."

She moves on to her next table on thick, short legs, dimpled with cellulite, rubber soles sliding across the ancient linoleum with an alternating slap and hiss.

"Look at this," Juan says, and he pulls up his pants leg to reveal a slick new plastic calf. "Went to Steamboat last month and got a replacement. Old one was starting to hurt if I walked too fast."

"Cool," Cole says, and Bridget puts a shining, triangular chip into the bowl of gooey salsa just to get her eye off of the leg.

"He gets around pretty good for a guy with a fake leg," she says when he moves on to the next table.

"Two of 'em. Both legs blown off above the knee more than twenty years ago at the Battle of Barbados," Cole says with quiet pride.

While they wait for their food Cole rolls out his plans to either get a two-year marriage deferment after high school or join straight up for a three-year hitch instead of waiting for his conscript papers. "There's a lot of advantages to joining right up. Like number one you get to request special assignments. Course I wouldn't mind going to one of the hotspots, like my Dad."

"You could get a tech support job, they have deferments."

"Yeah but you have to speak Mandarin. They don't even give it at our school. This one guy, Norris Allen, he got one of those jobs in Nevada but his Mom's Chinese so he speaks it okay. My Dad speaks some from when he was in service the first time but he never taught me. I'm thinking I might take a remote course in it."

Halfway through their meal an elderly couple enters and heads straight for the table. The man's joyful face and scalp are extraordinarily pink and shiny, like an uakari's, his lips and cheeks puffy and flushed; he looks like someone stuck a bicycle pump in his ear and inflated his head beyond its recommended p.s.i. The slender woman walking behind him wears an old-fashioned print dress and a pale straw hat, which she removes to reveal a head of graying brown hair pulled into a chignon. Like a lot of people around here, they look like they might have stepped out of a photograph from fifty years back, as content as if they had never heard of all the modern comforts the region lacks.

"Looks like Cole has a date, sweetie," the chipper old man says, wheezy and high-pitched. "You must be our wildlife biologist. I'm Dr. Edwin Glaspie and this is my wife, Liz."

"Bridget McCallum."

Glancing downward the doctor fails to hide his shock, and it takes her a moment to realize he's staring at her bottle of beer. When his eyes raise to her face again she takes a long swig and meets his gaze with a raised eyebrow.

"This is Dr. McCallum," Cole repeats helpfully, his ears so red they look like they've been boxed. "She's got a Ph.D. in biology."

The man's patient wife has quit pulling on his elbow. She stands behind him, miserably contemplating the imminent loss of the one free table in the restaurant as the door opens and a large woman in a black sweatsuit waddles toward it.

To Bridget's relief—she, too, mourning the missed opportunity with the table—the doctor now forces a grin and changes the subject. "Now tell me what you're doing up there?"

"Just checking up on the frogs."

"You know, we heard these same things about frogs a few years back, they were all going to disappear one day. Sure seem to be taking their time."

"They're doing okay up on that foothill."

"When your fieldwork is done I believe you'll find it's the water. Finest water in North America, pure snowmelt."

"There may be something to that," she says, though there isn't. "Cole was just telling me his father invented a desalinization process."

The doctor smiles indulgently at Cole, gives the boy's hair a patronizing tousle. "Well, he's a very smart man, Cole's Dad, but a little bit given to exaggeration. Let's say he wanted very badly to invent one."

Cole pipes up. "He said there wouldn't be anything to fight wars over anymore if there was a way to get everybody enough water."

The doctor eyes Cole as though calculating whether or not he's just been contradicted. "We've got enough here, unlike the rest of the West. You know Denver's dying to sell ours to those dirt farmers in Kansas. Those people'd love nothing more than getting our water, even if it means the people of Colorado go dry."

"I'm from Kansas," she says.

"It's no aspersion on the state. One of our boys lives in Wichita. Builds the big War Birds for the Armed Services."

Another table has opened up, and Mrs. Glaspie again takes her husband's elbow in her hand. "Eddie, there's our table. Very nice to have met you, Miss."

When they finish she calls for the check and discovers that Juan hasn't charged her for any of the beers. She pays with a voucher and leaves a cash tip for Sal who, Bridget now sees, is limping as she crosses the floor and could probably use a better break than an extra five dollars on top of the usual twenty percent.

Fridays the express shuttle leaves for Boulder. That morning she packs up water, algae, eggs, and larvae, each sample in its own plastic vial, into an insulated Styrofoam carrier which she seals with tape. With a marker she writes BIOLOGICAL SAMPLES DO NOT OPEN BIOHAZARD; this is untrue, but shuttle drivers have been known to open such packages scavenging for valuables or food.

The shuttle company on Second Street is manned by an earnest young man missing his left eye, the corresponding side of his face shiny with scar tissue in a radial starlike shape. He wears no cover over the eye, leaving the atrophied lids mostly closed over the dark, hollow socket; Bridget finds this strangely admirable and makes a point of looking him straight in the face.

"I need to send this to Boulder."

"That's a real Styrofoam cooler, isn't it?"

"I guess so. When will it get there?"

"Monday morning at the latest, barring breakdown or robbery."

"That's fine," she says, filling out an address form as he weighs the cooler.

On the wall is an out-of-date recruiting poster with the old slogan "Your Privilege to Serve," above a young white man in full body armor, his cruel jaw clamped tight. The corners of the poster are curling, with multiple pinholes surrounding the tacks that fix it to the wall behind the counter.

"Fifty-nine seventy-five," the clerk says.

"That's on the account of the State Department of Biological Affairs."

"You got to prove to me you're authorized, then."

She hands him her University and State IDs and authorization number, and after a show of skepticism he hands them back. "This stuff really biohazard?"

"Radioactive bearshit."

He clenches his jaw like the man in the poster and sets the package in an empty bin.

7

AFTER SCHOOL, Stacey stops by her daughter's worksite. Bee is framing a shed for Juan Stevens behind the restaurant, working without an assistant, and she doesn't stop hammering for her mother.

"What happened to Andy?"

"Got called up. Didn't you know? Left on yesterday's shuttle."

"He's asthmatic," she says, appalled. "One of his legs is shorter than the other."

"He'll lose one or the other before long anyway, and he can get a fake to match the one that's left," Bee says.

"Jesus, Bee, that's a kid we both know."

She shrugs. "He's the one who pointed it out. Look, I'm not happy about it, I could use some help, but he's probably better off leaving town."

"Unless he gets killed."

Her daughter shrugs. "Yeah, there's that."

Stacey wanders off in the direction of home feeling more alone than usual. Though she hates to admit it, her daughter and son are both corn-fed rubes, as their father used to call anyone born further than a hundred miles from an ocean; and while Buddy may have spent part of his youth in Chicago, and Juan Stevens in Kansas City, their conversations about their big city days revolve around live entertainment and the long-ago exploits of ball teams that don't even exist anymore.

Bridget's company is the only thing she looks forward to in the coming months; Buddy is going away with his loathsome wife Lena for two weeks on a city-funded trip to Santa Fe, the one place in the whole Mountain West that she still has any residual affection for. Not that she could have taken two weeks off school anyway, but the idea that the swinish Lena gets to make the trip with him makes her seethe.

The semester is off to a bad start as well; this year's freshman boys can be divided into three groups: zealots, thugs, and dolts. Several boys manage to straddle all three, terrorizing their less obviously pious classmates and once going so far as challenging Stacey's authority as an Episcopalian to teach Bible as History I. One of them drew an obscene picture of her in the boy's porta-john, on her knees with every orifice plugged and beads of sweat flying from her bobbing head. She interprets the drawing as an expression of contempt for her status as a divorcee (the fact that she is the only thrice-married member of the faculty, as noted in the school's annual report, has been much remarked on), rather than a declaration of desire. The days when she inspired flights of adolescent masturbatory fancy are gone, to her relief and slight regret. That she still has admirers closer to her own age—some of them persistent despite years of polite discouragement—in a town with a three to one ratio of women to healthy men, is good enough for Stacey.

And Buddy will do for the foreseeable future. He doesn't want more from her than to ravish her a couple of times a week, after which she cooks up some of the legally questionable, flashfrozen beef Buddy gets brought in from Denver. They accompany it with one or two of the finer selections from his clandestine wine stash, bottles confiscated years ago from the cellars of several wealthy absentee homeowners when the County Council—of which Buddy was a member—voted the county dry overnight.

They did it one November, with the town already unreachable through the snow, and those who returned after April's meltoff found the contents of their cellars seized as contraband. Back before the summer people had completely abandoned Gower, only a few of them understood how to deal profitably with Buddy. Those who demanded their property back, threatened legal action, or mentioned connections real or imagined with pols on the state or national stage were told that the bottles had been destroyed. Those, on the other hand, who elbowed Buddy and wondered aloud where in town to get a drink anymore had select bottles returned *gratis*, and some were even included in the loop when further skullduggery was being considered.

There were five councilmen back then, small business owners

all, and they each left office rich at a time when the opportunities for getting that way were disappearing along with those summer people. Besides losing their cellars, second homeowners were becoming disenchanted with the ever-shortening temperate season, reduced by then to four or five months. The year the first deep snowfall came at the start of September was the tipping point for most of them, and the following spring the melt came late too, in May. For Sale signs started going up, then Price Reduced signs, followed by Price Further Reduced.

In the end some of the summer houses were written off as losses, and a few locals got great deals on enormous houses, most of which were eventually abandoned as the cost of heating them soared ruinously high. And Buddy wound up with a world-class wine cellar underneath City Hall and practically no one but Stacey to share it with.

Arriving at the house she decides to hike up to see Bridget, but first she checks to make sure Cole is tending to the pony. Stacey finds him around the corner of the house, brushing its coat, lost as ever in thought of some unproductive kind; if he can harness some of that ruminative nature and apply it to some useful endeavor he may amount to something.

"When you're done with Mysti I'd like you to mow the grass around the house."

He nods. "Okay."

His lack of resistance is novel, but she'll take what she can get. "Thanks."

"Stacey, do you think Lamar might be out somewhere, hurt?"

"If he was hurt bad enough to still be out there he'd be dead, I think."

"Maybe he got conscripted like Dad. Maybe he ran away."

"You know, Cole, what I really think happened is he got busted for shooting his mouth off all the time. Maybe killed."

Cole looks so shocked she feels bad, but surely this isn't the first time the thought has crossed his mind. Though everyone she knows feels ghastly about it, particularly for Gail and the girls, no one is surprised.

Cole is crying, his face gone puffy in the space of an instant, rivulets wetting the peachfuzz on his cheeks. She grabs him and holds him for a minute, rocking him in a way she hasn't since the first year or so after she married Ted, feeling for once like a mother to him.

He calms down quickly and she pulls away to avoid embarrassing him any further. "I'm going to hike up to Bridget's camp," she says, and his disappointed, left-out look is so pathetic and ingenuous she throws him a bone. "When you're done with the grass why don't you come up and join us."

"Okay." The boy nods and looks over at the pony.

She starts up the foothill road making a conscious effort to savor the feel of the air, hot but still invigorating rather than stifling. That won't last more than another week or so, and when the summer doldrums hit with full force she'll be stuck inside with the windows wide open and the fans running day and night, except on the bike to and from school.

By the time the road has climbed to the plateau the air is cooler by ten or fifteen degrees at least. For a minute she wishes she were young, with some sort of interesting career ahead of her, and nothing to tie her to Gower. Winter is bad enough, but every year when that blazing rough patch arrives in July and August she thinks hard about writing the ranch off as a total loss—she hates to think what she could have sold it for when her father died, when the tourist industry was still hanging in, at least in summer—and moving someplace where a patina of civilization still faintly shines.

When she gets to camp Bridget isn't there, nor is her gearbag. Stacey takes the folding chair in front of the tent and carries it to a shady spot overlooking the pond. She takes the crumbling paperback novel out of her pack and sits down to read.

When she wakes to the sound of voices the sun is almost behind the mountain, with a small amount of direct sunlight burning the peaks on the opposite side of the valley a pinkish orange, which makes it five or later. She stares into the sky, trying to recapture the wisp of an interrupted dream, the lingering warmth of it teasing her until it pops back into focus: she was dreaming of Ted, a happy dream, and the pleasant feeling turns to resentment at his ability to colonize her subconscious and make her forget how much he's fucked up her life.

Cole is sitting crosslegged next to Bridget in front of her tent, and she rises to join them. Lugging the chair over her shoulder, she tries not to look pissed off.

"How long was I asleep?"

"I got back at three and you were out," Bridget says. "I didn't have the heart to wake you up."

"You should have, I came up just to see you." In her groggy disappointment she's unable to keep a bitchy note out of her voice. "Now I'll never sleep tonight."

"Sorry."

"Forget it, I probably needed it anyway."

"Nice day for it," Bridget says.

"What have you two been talking about?"

For the first time Cole glances up at her from the corner of his eye a little smirk on his lips. "Talking about me maybe spending the night up here this weekend."

"He says he likes to camp out," Bridget says. "Can't stand it, myself, but I don't mind having some company up here."

"That's nice," Stacey says. "Maybe I'll come with you."

Cole, who hasn't found his poker face yet and may never have one, looks aghast. She understands and relents. "Or maybe I'll do it some other weekend."

"That's fine, too," Bridget says. She actually winks at her, for no reason Stacey can understand, and then it occurs to her that this invitation to Cole is meant as a favor to her and not the boy.

And so on Friday night Stacey plays hostess to her ex-husband, his honor the mayor of Gower. He arrives in the Municipal Van, which blows up such a cloud of dust and smoke on the county road she curses his lack of discretion and common sense in not riding a bicycle over the way anybody else would have done. When he stops in front of the house and asks if she wants him to park it out back out of sight she turns and goes into the house without a word, leaving him to guess what he's done wrong.

The two dusty bottles of turn-of-the century Chateau Margaux he carries by the neck go a long way toward forgiveness. Buddy doesn't give a shit about wine except as a commodity, but likes owning something so many other people want. He's proud of the fact that he took every bottle in his cellar by force from people who were richer and more powerful—or so they thought—than he, but his contraband beverage of choice is beer.

Since she can't come close to affording the beef Buddy feeds her—one of their meals in his office would cost her two weeks' salary—Stacey grills a couple of thawed out venison steaks bought from Rex Daggett and they eat them accompanied by the first bottle of Margaux. She'd never admit it to Buddy, who sees her as the embodiment of worldliness, but Stacey never knows what she should be tasting for in a forty-year-old bottle of wine other than whether it's gone obviously skunky. She loves the wine, though, and she improvises an appreciation that's half sincere and half bullshit: cherry, tobacco, leather, chitin, shredded newsprint. Buddy agrees, tearing into his meat and nodding as he chews.

He has a fresh haircut, which she appreciates (though she wonders who cut it), and wears a shirt she hasn't seen before that's wrong for him, a shade of lilac that doesn't go with his big green eyes, once his most attractive trait; with the weight he's gained in the last few years, though, they've started to look wet and bulbous, and bold colors draw attention to them and how fast he's aging.

A half hour after the last scraps of the venison have been consumed he's huffing and puffing atop her as she thinks, despite herself, of that second bottle of Margaux. After Buddy ejaculates, with his usual melodramatic torso-stiffening and the weird, loud deflation of his lungs that she once imagined were meant for comic effect, he lays there panting for a minute or so, then speaks. "It still feels weird on Ted's bed, right in his house."

"It's my house and my bed, not Ted's."

"Baby, according to the laws of the state of Colorado it's his house as much as it is yours."

"And Ted took off, so you've got no business worrying about him."

"I'm not worried." He lays back and pouts, looking at the ceiling. "I'm just saying it feels weird."

"Hey." She rises up onto her elbows. "Is there any way you could find out where he is?"

"Nope."

"I know you know somebody in Denver who knows somebody in Washington. And they could just tell you if he's really in the Service."

"I can't think of a better way to fuck up my beautiful easy existence than to start pestering the Feds about a soldier they plainly don't want me to know about. Who cares, anyway?"

She rises up on her elbows. "He's my husband, Buddy."

"I just mean if he got shanghaied by a contractor or the military, those guys never come back, almost. And if he ran out on you why would you even want him to come back?"

"Because I want a divorce."

Buddy looks away, toward the door. "I mean, both of us being married kind of works out even, doesn't it?"

"Jesus, Buddy, I'm not asking you to get one. I just don't like being married to a guy who's not around."

Buddy let's out something like a sigh. "If he hadn't been a fucking technical wizard he would've been the worst employee I ever had."

"Knock it off, he kept you in business for years."

"You're defending him now?"

"Just giving him his due," she says, wondering where this protective feeling came from. "That's why they took him, you know."

"Who took who?"

"That's why the Feds took Ted. They're always short of competent tech monkeys." She rests her head on her crossed arms, guilty and sad for a moment. She knows it's true, that Ted might have abandoned her but not the boy, and here she is cavorting in their bed with her ex-husband, his former boss. Oh, well, she thinks. Can't be helped.

Back in the living room she fires up the television and opens a bottle of beer for Buddy without mentioning the other bottle of Margaux. They start watching a movie, a docudrama about the infiltration of the California State University system by subversives.

She's engrossed in the melodramatics of the plot and only half-aware of Buddy's presence next to her when, to her considerable surprise, he cups his right hand over her left breast and after a moment's perfunctory fondling, sticks his hand inside her robe and starts rolling the nipple back and forth.

"What the hell, Buddy, I'm watching the movie."

"It's a piece of shit. And who knows when we'll get a chance to do it in a bed next?"

He takes her hand and places it on his crotch. "You just did it an hour ago. How can you want to again?"

"I took a pill."

She's shocked. He's never needed to resort to pharmaceuticals. "Really? Is everything okay down there?"

"I didn't need it the first time. I took it when the movie started."

She holds her breath, lets it out slowly. "What kind?"

"Euphoria, hallucinations. Yellow, diamond-shaped."

"I don't know the shapes by heart, Buddy."

"Starts with an *F*. The kind where your cock starts to hurt like hell if you don't come within an hour or two."

"Jesus, Buddy. Didn't they outlaw those?"

He nods, looking down at the floor like a student caught in an infraction, guilty and appealing for undeserved clemency.

"All right. I'm tempted to make you suffer through it for not telling me in advance, but come on." She leads him back to the conjugal bed he's so excited about defiling.

It's quick and frantic this time, but he seems to enjoy himself tremendously. "I should be careful," he says afterward, flat on his back and gulping huge lungfuls of the closed bedroom's stale air. "Those boner pills'll give you a heart attack if you don't watch out."

"You could stand to lose thirty pounds, sugar," she says. She almost never criticizes him—he doesn't take it well—but lying there wheezing, forehead slick with sweat, he looks like another five minutes might have sent him over.

"Well, they ought to come up with something non-lethal. It's a good high, though, I can see why they were popular."

"Make a better boner pill and the world will beat a path to your door."

"Yeah." He stares at the ceiling.

"Nice haircut, by the way."

"Thanks," he says. "Greta did it. Going to be a good skill to have around here if we keep losing our haircare professionals."

This touches a nerve with her, since she's always a little nervous that her daughter Bee and her lady friend are going to be taken away some dark night to a sexual reorientation camp just like poor Ivan the hairdresser last year. But it also brings to mind something she wants Buddy to stay on top of. "Poor Lamar. Did you know the Feds are trying to squeeze Gail and the girls out of their house?"

"Yep." He closes his eyes.

"Do you think you could step in and stop it?"

"Babe, this is the second time tonight you've asked me to annoy dear old Uncle Sam about someone he clearly doesn't want to be asked about."

"I'm not asking you to intervene for Lamar, he's a lost cause anyway. Do it for the girls."

He sighs, pinches the bridge of his nose and opens his rheumy eyes. "There's a story going around about some Homeland Security contractors getting ambushed and killed trying to bring him down."

"You don't believe that."

"I don't, but it makes me think the Feds are real serious about whatever they busted him on."

The movie is over when they leave the bedroom, stiff and sore and out of sorts. He pours himself another beer and scowls at the next feature, an old one about friendly aliens that she remembers watching on TV as a small child, redone now with modern, hyper-realistic special effects that kill all her nostalgic pleasure in the thing.

"I ought to get you a better set than this."

"This one's okay. Signal here is shit most of the time, anyway, thanks to you, Jason. Anyway those big sets use too much juice."

"Don't call me Jason." He hasn't used his real name, not even on the ballot, since a fraternity brother renamed him after a comic book character thirty-odd years ago. "I ought to get you some bigger panels and a better battery. You'd be surprised how much you can store with these new ones."

"I can't afford them and you shouldn't give them to me. It'd look bad when Lena divorces you."

When Buddy leaves she can hear the Municipal Van inside the house with the doors closed, a noise like the sound of a playing card being flapped by the spokes of a bicycle, only raucous and loud and vaguely flatulent. If the whole valley didn't know before what she and Buddy were up to they must now. She supposes Cole and Bridget must have heard it up at the lake.

Before bed she calls up an old message, the one announcing Ted's conscription, its salutation throbbing from red to white to blue against a similarly shifting background:

> GREETINGS!
>
> We are proud to inform you that your loved one Elder Theodore H. has elected to serve in one of his Country's Armed Services. Rest assured that his safety and well-being are our paramount concern.
>
> Yours,
>
> William Kader,
>
> Acting Superintendent, Recruitment Division

It certainly looks like one of those letters they send as a kind of half-assed apology when they shanghai someone, but you can't trace government i-messages, not legally anyway, not without inviting a visit from a security contractor. Anyway Ted of all people would have known how to fake the thing.

She cleans up the kitchen and folds the TV screen. She scrubs her face and, climbing into bed, discovers that the sheets smell like Buddy, his familiar, not unpleasant mix of sweat and cologne mingled with something new and jarring, probably something hormonal from the boner pill. She goes upstairs to the guest room instead.

8

ON THE FOURTH OF JULY Bridget bikes into town to watch fire-works from the rooftop of Consuela's. The restaurant below is closed for the night, since Juan insists that it's wrong to make money off of the national holiday. Besides, there's free shitty food being given away on Second Street, and who is she, anyway, to question the patriotic authority of a man who gave both his legs in service of his country? He makes an impressive show of leading the way up the aluminum ladder in a pair of short pants. A cooler of beer and a wicker basket of food follow on a pulley, and they sit on blankets laid over the flat gravel roof, eating fried rabbit and sipping cold beer.

Stacey's son Leo sits with his long, ungainly legs crossed atop an ancient, rusted-over condenser unit with half its wiring sticking out of its crumpled aluminum cover. Leo's ignoring the spectacle of Juan flirting with his mother, and for the first time Bridget thinks she might make time with one of the locals. He's not very exciting, Leo, but he's reasonably educated and within a stone's throw of handsome, and Stacey has more than once suggested they spend some time together.

Before the first rocket bursts Stacey's already grousing about the dangers. "When I lived in California you had to be a licensed pyrotechnician to put on a show like this. Every damn Fourth of July some bonehead somewhere would start a brush fire and burn a subdivision down to the ground."

"Babe, that was another place and another time," Juan says.

"Fire's fire, and idiots shooting off fireworks are idiots shooting off fireworks."

Juan scarcely gets off the first syllables of a reply when a dull report booms in the distance, followed by a trail of orange sparks surging upward, and the five of them watch in silence until it bursts into a shimmering, crackling lavender blossom, upon which they voice a chorus of inarticulate moans specific to fireworks shows.

"There's not much of a fire hazard," Juan argues once the spectacle has faded away. "They've never set a building on fire yet."

"As opposed to people," she says as an orchid burst blooms overhead, its tail spattering fading sparks onto the river below.

"That's not fair. That was a goddamn tragedy and nobody's fault."

Leo brightens and half-grins. He has a moustache that Bridget finds mildly repulsive, curling over his lower lip and most of the time obscuring his mouth, an affectation that might be an impediment to the most casual of summer affairs. "Fire Chief peeled the paper wrap off the top of a big boxful of rockets, supposed to keep 'em from all going off at once, and as soon as they lit the first one that's what they did."

Juan nods. "Shots going off left and right, rockets and Roman candles all going up at the same time, a hell of a lot of racket. The crowd thought it was part of the show, they were all going nuts cheering it on. One of the Brigade tried to put it out before the whole riverbank caught fire, and the poor fucker got burned so bad he croaked a week after."

"That's awful."

Stacey shakes her head. "And these are the guys who are putting on tonight's show."

"Be fair," Juan says. "They all took a remote course in fireworks safety."

Another sparkler rises, followed by two more, all three giving off showers of purple sparks. When they detonate in the air and separate into tiny starbursts, popping and whistling, everyone stops talking for a minute.

Bridget wonders aloud how the town can afford such an elaborate display. "TarMart," Stacey says. "When they sponsor the Fourth of July bash in these mountain towns where they can only do business in summertime, their sales go up something like fifteen or twenty percent. People forget they were mad at them all winter about their broken appliances and crappy furniture."

The carousing on the streets below is getting louder, the sounds of celebration bacchanalian and sloppy, and before the fireworks have ended a drunk pounds on the front door of the restaurant, demanding to be let in and fed. Juan leans over the edge of the rooftop and calls down to the man.

"Freddy, man, we're closed for the Fourth. There's hot dogs and soyburgers on Second in front of the old courthouse."

"I don't want that shit," Freddy says, out of Bridget's line of sight.

He sounds fat, though, and he slurs so badly she pictures him in a top hat, woozily holding onto the base of a lamppost, with cartoon Xs for eyes and a bright red nose. "Want a fuckin' enchilada."

"Aren't any to be had. Cook's got the day off."

The drunk goes back to pounding the door, then starts pounding on the glass of the front window. Juan's getting agitated now.

"Goddamnit, Freddy, stop hitting my window. You can't afford to replace it and neither can I."

The pounding continues, the window vibrating like a washtub and sounding perilously close to shattering.

"You hit that window once more and I'm coming down after you."

The next blow to the window sounds.

To Bridget's astonishment, and Stacey's eye-rolling disdain, Juan drops off the edge of the roof. He's standing up straight when he goes over, and Bridget scrambles over to the ledge for a look; below, Juan is already pounding on a supine Freddy, who isn't fat at all, not even pudgy.

"He's always doing that," Stacey says. "The jumping off the roof thing, he thinks it's impressive."

"I'd sure like a pair of legs like that someday," Cole says, and

Leo snickers when in sharp unison both women snap at him in contradiction.

Leo falls in alongside her on the way back to the bicycles.

"How'd an able-bodied guy like you manage to get out of national service intact?" Bridget asks.

"I served two tours in Homeland Relief." His tone is apologetic.

"Just a little defensive, huh?"

"My ex-stepdad pulled a few strings. I never saw any action worse than a hurricane or an earthquake."

"Which hurricane?"

"I was in Galveston for Theodosia and Boston for Nathaniel. And Los Angeles after Studio City."

That sounds almost as bad as combat to Bridget, who nods.

"I just put in a new satellite receiver," he goes on. "Got a nice big screen and better reception than anybody in town. City paid for it, since I have to get legal stuff from Denver on it all the time."

"Good for you," she says.

"It's not so special," Cole says.

"I thought maybe you'd like to watch a movie or something. Let me know. I could show you anything you wanted. Old or new."

"Maybe sometime," she says. Stacey looks back over her shoulder at the three of them.

"I don't know why you'd want to watch a movie in a cramped little office," Cole says.

The next day Bridget's inputting the day's notes when she hears a loud noise in the distance. She stands to see over the top of her tent and sees Rex Daggett with his long blond braids coiled on the sides of his head now like a little Swiss girl.

"Brought you a present," he calls, holding a dripping burlap sack in his enormous left hand, which he raises for her to see, very pleased with himself.

She wonders if this is a form of rural courtship, wonders too whether he has a wife who does those braids. "What do you have?"

"Something weird."

She's guessing it's going to be an albino, or a few adults with malformed or extra limbs, expectations so low that when he opens the bag and spills its slippery contents onto the grass she jumps back in shock.

"You ever seen one like that before?"

She most certainly has not: dead tadpoles, morphologically identical as far as she can see to *Rana catesbeiana* larvae, only between six and twelve inches long. Seeing no signs of metamorphosis she crouches to touch one, still slick with mucous; it can't have been dead long. The head is as big as her fist, and looks to have been a healthy specimen, apart from having grown to this size without growing legs or losing its tail. "Where'd you find these?"

"Stinky little pond, sits next to the old mine pit. It's full of the damned things."

"Any of them have legs?"

"None I saw. And I'll tell you something else, it's the first time I seen anything alive in there. Got all kinds of chemicals and shit in it."

"This the molybdenum mine?"

"Naw, this is an old-time mine. Copper. Played out maybe eighty, ninety years ago."

"I've never seen anything like these."

"You think the government did it? 'Cause that's what I been hearing for years, is the Feds did this to the frogs to see what happens."

"Don't be a dope. The government's spending a lot of money trying to stop these kinds of things."

"That don't mean they didn't do it. I also heard they kill whole ponds worth of fish and frogs and shit when their experiments don't turn out right."

"So where is this pit?"

"You go five miles south on the county road, then there's a little dirt road that's state property, says no trespassing but you don't need to bother with that. Quite a ways down the dirt road into the valley's the lake. I'll take you there if you like."

"Could we go tomorrow?"

"All right. You just meet me out on the county road, out where the old filling station is."

When he's out of sight she logs on and notifies the department in Boulder about the freaks and her plans to investigate. She hears back immediately; she's to ship the anomaly on the next shuttle for analysis, a rapid enough response to give her pause.

Getting to the lake at the mine pit is a good deal more difficult than she imagined, hiking for three or four miles alongside what was once a major paved road, now reduced to enormous shards

of asphalt thrown from the ground as if by eons of seismic disturbance, though in fact the road was only decommissioned in the
late 1960s. This history comes from Rex, who bounds from one
chunk of broken pavement to the next with childish pleasure while
Bridget struggles to keep up on the flat grass beside him. It's only
nine in the morning and the day is just going to get worse. Better
to move quickly while they can.

At a low spot in the valley, the landscape is dominated for a
quarter mile or so by the wooden and concrete shells of buildings,
skeletal remains of the mountain hamlet that serviced the mine.

"Mine stopped producing in the nineteen-fifties and they
just let the town go all to hell. Purdy, it was called. Eventually
everybody'd either died or left. People'd come and squat around
here 'cause nobody wanted the land, but they never lasted long.
Cancers and goiters. Kids born with tails. Shit like that."

"Really?"

"No shit, I had kin tried to live around here a few years back.
Cousin of mine dropped out a kid with a tail six inches long. He
could wag it, too. Thought it'd keep him out of the Service, but he
got picked up anyway, got killed over in the Solomons. That was
a shame, 'cause he was the only one of hers that come out alive at
all." Rex quiets down for a few paces, then turns back to her. "You
know this pond's been here next to the pit the whole time and I
never saw anything alive in it. Don't come out here much since
there's not much to shoot and what you do shoot you might not
want to eat."

"What brought you here the other day, then?"

He glances at her over his shoulder and doesn't answer.

"Sorry," she says.

The road comes to an old fence topped with rusted razor wire and a gate long ago busted through, a guard station sitting dilapidated just beyond. She peers into it as they pass by, disappointed not to find a uniformed skeleton bravely manning its post.

"Not far now," Rex says.

She winces at a smell like battery acid and sulfur, realizes it's been teasing her nostrils for a mile or two. Now it overpowers the odor of pine and stings her sinuses just behind her eyes. "Jesus," she says, stopping and holding her palms over her nose.

"Pretty, ain't it." Rex takes in a loud lungful, lets it out as though deciphering its bouquet. "Believe that sharp smell's selenium. Used to use that to tone photographic paper. Bet you didn't know that."

There are two filtration units in her pack, and fastening hers around the back of her head and over her face she wishes she'd thought to wear it from the start of the hike. Rex looks puzzled when she holds the second unit out for him.

"It's a chemical filter."

"Little smell don't bother me."

"You really don't want this stuff in your lungs."

"I been breathing that shit for years. Another afternoon's worth won't make any difference one way or the other."

Bridget keeps holding the unit out for him to grab, and finally he laughs and moves on. She puts his filter back into its case and slips it into her pack, hoping he's right.

Past the gate the grasses start to thin out and the trees are fewer and sparser. Dead ones abound, and though she hasn't heard a bird in a while she can't say exactly when they stopped, and hot and wet though it is the scene has the feel of dry winter.

"Back in the teens they were going to spend a whole shitload of money cleaning it up," Rex says. "Didn't do fuck-all about it, though, government ran out of money. Eventually they just padlocked the place and figured anybody stupid enough to come around here deserves whatever they get." He stops to pick up a flat stone and throws it into a copse of dead, gray trees, one of which cracks when it hits. "Guess that's you and me."

"Guess so," she says, self-conscious about the sound of her voice through the mask, her breath coming back to her sour and muggy.

There's nothing left to see of the mine but the pit itself, a quarter of a mile in diameter, which at first glance appears lifeless. A hundred yards to the east of it sits a pond about the size of Stacey's, and when they get closer an enormous freak tadpole leaps out of the water like a footlong orca, twisting in the air seemingly for the pure pleasure of it.

"There's your freaks, right there," Rex says, and spits. "I got me some business to tend to not far from here. I'll be back in about an hour if you want me to walk you back to the county road." He disappears into the woods, cracking dried branches underfoot for a minute or so before the sound fades to nothing.

Donning an elbow-length pair of work gloves she telescopes the collection net and in the space of fifteen minutes she's collected three specimens even larger than the one Rex brought her, each sealed in a plastic pouch filled with clear preservative gel. She takes water samples from all sides of the pond and then, very carefully, repeats the process at the pit itself. It bubbles nastily at its north shore, with a rainbow slick at the top and a phosphorescent orange tint. Checking the database this morning she wasn't able to find a soil analysis later than the nineteen-eighties for the site, or an atmospheric later than the turn of the century, and as far as she can tell no one's ever sampled the water from the pit. It's not even clear anymore whose land this is, so zestfully did the federal, state and county governments and the mining company flee their respective liabilities. She made note of that fact in her communications with the department and received in return a caution from her supervisor not to do anything that might interfere with a possible University claim on the land.

A couple of hours have passed and Rex isn't back from whatever his *sub rosa* business was. She heads up toward the county road, shoulder harness fully loaded. When she gets back to the main road and her bike it's an hour's ride into Gower, and when she steps into the shuttle office the same clerk, wearing a patch over the empty socket today, is hard at work sealing a package. Above him, a portrait of the mayor like the one at Consuela's beams out, following Bridget with his gaze as she approaches the desk.

"Hi, Bob."

He looks up, startled, and then looks down at his nametag. Mystery solved. He scowls when she presents him with a pair of Styrofoam carriers marked BIOHAZARD—THIS IS CONTAM-INATED—DANGER. He squints at them with his one eye then looks back up at Bridget.

"I'm not sure we're authorized to ship this kind of thing if it's contaminated."

"State Department of Biological Affairs."

"I know, but the driver bitched an awful lot the last time about that bearshit of yours."

"Tell him not to be a pussy. As long as he doesn't open them up he'll be fine," she says, hoping it's true. She and Bob are still going round and round about it five minutes later when a family group comes through the door. "Shit," he says. "You win. I got to take care of somebody." He writes up the manifest and sets it onto the pallet with a the put-upon look of a one-eyed man at a disadvantage. "Afternoon, Mr. Mayor," he says.

"Afternoon, Robert." He leans down on the counter and talks to Bob in a voice too low for Bridget to catch, this guy who's got Stacey climbing the walls. His eyes are bulging green and watery, and he persists in snorting something back in his sinuses until finally he swallows whatever it was, kicking at Bob's counter absently with a loafer that looks to Bridget like real leather.

The ride back leaves her caked with dusty sweat. At camp it's at least ten degrees cooler than down below, but that's small relief to her as she sets her bike next to the tent and walks to the creek, where she peels off her clothes and steps into the cold flowing water. The bottom isn't muddy, mostly stones rounded smooth over the years, the water just over two feet deep. It's so cold at first she almost gives up, but shortly she's accustomed to it and submerged, her hair loose and wet.

As an idea strikes, Bridget rises and carries her clothes over to the ancient wooden dock that juts ten feet into the pond. Stepping gingerly to avoid splinters she walks to the end of the dock; the ladder leading off of it is disintegrating, so she cannonballs into her research project, disturbing several hundred of her subjects and getting a mouthful of muddy water in the process. She spends a few minutes swimming underwater in the manner of a frog, stopping, kicking, stopping, kicking; she floats on her back and practices all the strokes she can remember from childhood. Then she swims back and forth across the pond until she loses count of the number of laps. Then more floating on her back, lapsing into a half-sleeping state, which comes abruptly to an end when she hears her name called.

She submerges and then rises again, only her head poking above the water. It's Cole, standing on the dock, looking first at her and then at the pile of clothes, seemingly putting the puzzle together very, very slowly.

"Are you *naked*?" Scandalized, he looks at her and away and back. "You shouldn't swim naked."

"Why not?"

Thinking hard: "Nobody does that."

"Turn around and I'll get out."

The decrepit ladder isn't an option for exiting the water, and she can't shinny up the rough gray pylons without cutting her hands. This leaves two options: having Cole pull her out of the water stark-ass naked onto the dock, or walking out onto the muddy bank and run the risk of disturbing an egg clutch. She chooses the latter option and walks onto shore, a slippery mass of tadpoles wriggling about her feet. She dries herself off with her shirt and puts on her underwear and shorts; Cole will have to deal with seeing her in a wet t-shirt.

"Okay."

He turns to look and whips his head away while she walks to the tent. She grabs a bright green, dry tank top from the tent and slips it on. "Okay, I'm dressed."

He turns to face her but can't quite manage to look at her face. "Something bad's the matter with Stacey."

In the house she finds Stacey lying on her bed in a fetal position, clutching her belly and moaning, semiconscious. "Call a doctor," she tells Cole.

"How?"

She struggles to stay patient. "On the phone."

"I'm not allowed."

"Not allowed?"

"Phone's too expensive. Only her and my Dad's allowed."

"Cole, this is an emergency."

He stands there without speaking, lower lip slack with indecision, and for the first time she speaks sharply to him. "Damn it, go phone a doctor."

"I don't know how," he blurts.

She looks around the screen for it and doesn't find one connected. "Do you even have one?" she asks.

He opens a cabinet along the wall where an old handset phone lies unused, unconnected to the screen, its charge completely down. "All right, I'm going to ride into town and bring one back. Where should I go? Who should I ask for?"

"Dr. Glaspie."

"Dr. Glaspie the vet?"

The sun is low in the sky when she gets into town. The Glaspies live in a two-story house, its green paint battered by years of extreme weather. Mrs. Glaspie greets her with studied gentility and the doctor, called away from the composition of a sermon, greets Bridget with a sigh.

"What, Miss McCallum?"

"Stacey Elder's real sick."

"What's the matter with her?"

"Something abdominal. She's incoherent."

"All right," he says, and he returns to the door a moment later with a bigger medical bag than she's ever seen. "Will you ride with me in the Municipal Van or on your bike?"

"Bike," she says.

She can hear the sprockety sound of the Municipal Van long after it's out of sight, and smell it too. Apart from that the ride back to the house is almost bearable, the breeze having cooled somewhat and the adrenaline from the scare having worn off. When she gets to the house Cole is sitting at the table reading a school-book. "What's he say?"

"Nothing."

She pokes her head into the room. Stacey is lying flat on her back, eyes closed, but her face isn't contorted as before. The doctor—she hates to think of him as the vet—is seated at Stacey's side, and looks up at her. "It's her appendix. You were right to come and get me."

"What do you do for that?"

"Antibiotics. If we were in a city they'd do it laparoscopically, probably, but that's not one of our options so we'll just have to make do with what we've got. Now this one's only available in its veterinary form as an injectable. I presume you can give an injection?"

"No. But I guess I can if I have to."

"Don't worry, Cole can do it. Cole! Come in here."

Cole peeks in around the door, only his head visible. "Yes sir?"

"You're going to be injecting your stepmother twice a day for the next three days. Can you handle that?"

"Uh-huh."

"Don't say *uh-huh*, boy, you sound like a monkey."

"Yes sir."

By evening the family has arrived, and Cole plays a complicated game of tag with Stacey's granddaughter Nina. Leo spends forty-five minutes inside with his mother and sister, then comes outside to talk to Bridget.

"Do you know Cole doesn't know how to use the phone?"

"Doesn't surprise me," he says.

"It wasn't even charged up."

"My Mom gets a little lax about things sometimes," Leo says. "Thanks for helping out today."

"That's okay."

"We should have dinner sometime. You think?"

"Yeah, maybe, when things quiet down a little around here."

Once he's pedaled away the daughter comes out of the house, looking chipper. "She's a little better already. Can't be the antibiotics yet. I halfway think it's just a bug anyway, not appendicitis. What's Glaspie know, anyway?"

Nina clings to her mother's leg and whines to go home. "You're going home with Unca Leo, sweetheart. Momma's going to stay here and take care of Goomah tonight."

"I can stay tonight," Bridget says when Nina's little chin quivers on the brink of a keening wail. "Go on home. I can fix Cole some dinner, then I'll sit up late with Stacey."

Nina is already over at the bicycles, waiting for one of the adults to get into the front seat so she can hop onto the back. "Okay. I'll ride back out tomorrow."

Before dinner she sets the phone onto its charger, verifies that the latter is connected to the house's main battery, and explains to Cole how it works.

"How did you get to be almost seventeen without a phone? Every kid in Boulder has one from the age of, like, five."

"But you're on the Big Grid there. Nobody's got one here," he says, not as defensive as she would have been at his age. "We don't get much feed except in the afternoon."

"You have a land line."

"The land line's real expensive. That's why I'm not allowed."

While Stacey sleeps and Cole watches a war movie she suspects Stacey would have forbidden, she showers, lathering her hair for the first time in over a week. She's half-convinced the mine pit odor clings to it like a shroud, wonders if an odor can lodge in your brain permanently.

When she's done she goes downstairs and finds Cole sitting alone on the couch, the screen off.

"Is your movie over?" she asks.

"I quit watching. You always know what's going to happen in these war movies."

"I guess I don't watch them very often."

"I can tell you at the beginning who's going to live and who's going to die every time. I stopped this one when this one foreigner they took prisoner cut the sergeant's throat with a plastic spork. I knew that sergeant was a goner first time he was onscreen."

"Maybe we can watch something after dinner and you can demonstrate."

After a dinner of Stacey's leftover squirrel rillettes on toast they watch the only thing on offer that neither of them has seen, a horror picture about a girls' boarding school, and Cole's predictions regarding the characters' varied fates are remarkably accurate. "Chemistry teacher's the killer," he says, fifteen minutes in.

"Killer's a man, they're sex killings."

"She's a homosexual. They're always the killer. You watch."

By the end of the picture he's proved right, the nefarious Sapphic chemist awaiting the needle, and every character whose demise Cole predicted, dead.

9

SHORTLY AFTER DAYBREAK is the only pleasant time for bike riding in the summer, and Dr. Glaspie takes his time, enjoying the morning smells that the heat will have drowned out by nine. At the Elder ranch he finds Stacey with her fever broken, coherent and able to sit up. He'll still be taking over her classes himself for a few days, and he extracts from her a distracted précis of her lesson plans for the rest of the week, plans he suspects her of improvising on the spot.

On his way out the McCallum girl stops him. He finds her presence distracting, not because of her youth and attractiveness—he has to deal with the lissome Karen Ingelblad on a daily basis, after all—but because she doesn't seem to think she owes him any kind of deference. Ever mindful and wary of the dangers of pride, he's nonetheless accustomed to outward shows of respect from the locals. This one talks to him as though he were some random old man with no authority over her, moral or otherwise.

This morning, though, she surprises him with her downcast, supplicant air as she nearly genuflects, asking his permission to leave Stacey Elder alone. "I'm supposed to go to the old Purdy pit this morning, but I'll postpone it if Stacey needs me to stay."

That she's prepared to leave her sick friend alone for the day for the sake of a nature hike sickens him. Stacey would stay home if their situations were reversed. "If your hike is so important to you, I suppose you should go ahead and do it."

"It's not a hike, it's research. And anyway, her daughter's coming out sometime today."

Her upper incisors are large and prominent, which leads to a slight, habitual parting of the lips, and for an unguarded instant he thinks she's lucky to have escaped the orthodontia that would have ruined that beguiling half-smile. "Purdy's not easy to find anymore. The road's not marked."

"I've already been. Rex Daggett took me."

"Rex Daggett? You should be careful around the Daggetts."

"Why?"

Is this willful obtuseness or is she genuinely stupider than he'd pegged her for? "The Daggetts deal in illegal goods, particularly contraband meat. They're poachers, I know that for certain, and I suspect they're involved in supplying drugs up at the mine. Voltamine, plus that stuff the city kids call Wighat, as well as various hallucinogens."

"I really have to go up there, whether it's today or some other day." She has a low, suggestive voice that would have been described in his youth as smoky, though he sees no other evidence of the sins of the tobacco field.

"Then may as well make it today." He calls upstairs. "Cole, will you ride to school with me?"

"I don't have to be there until ten today," Cole yells back.

"Nonsense. There's plenty to be done in the morning before classes. Have you cared for the pony?"

"Yes sir."

"Then finish getting dressed and come along."

Miss Ingelblad is in her Quonset hut when they arrive.

"Good morning, Karen."

She looks up from her reading, making no effort to mask her annoyance at its interruption. "Hello. Cole, maybe you can help Dr. Glaspie in the office until class time," she says.

Dr. Glaspie steps behind her desk to read over her shoulder. He's gratified to see that she's halfway through Halley's "Archeological Perspectives on the Bible," a book he presented to the school himself. "Reading up on Jonah?"

"Uncovering the Walls of Jericho. Wrapped Jonah up a couple of weeks ago."

"Good. Well, I'll take our Cole out to the office and set him to work there. Carry on."

The corners of her mouth crease upward for a millisecond's acknowledgment before her eyes return to the page.

In the office he makes a pot of chicory and instructs the boy to sit and read his assignments for the day. He wishes he'd simply ordered Miss Ingelblad to keep the boy in her classroom, but he feels some responsibility in the matter, having strong-armed the boy into coming.

"What's Miss McCallum doing up there, anyway?"

"Studying the frogs and tadpoles."

"No, I mean exactly?"

"She's using her camera and counting them and doing..." He falters.

"Is she doing something wrong, Cole?"

"No."

"Then what is it you don't want to say?"

"She's doing a study on their"—his voice constricts, pops an octave, drops again—"their DNA." He looks down at his history book.

"What's the matter with that?"

"Remember what you said."

"About what?"

"About there's no such thing as DNA."

"I never said that, Cole. There's such a thing as DNA."

The boy looks confused and slightly frightened, as if he's being subjected to a loyalty test of some sort. "I thought you said there wasn't."

"I said genetics doesn't prove evolution. Every time they try to defend their theory they use DNA. I just want you to think critically when you hear about things like that."

"Oh. Well, then that's what she's doing."

"And she's pretty good friends with your stepmother?"

"Yeah, pretty good."

"How's she doing otherwise?"

"Stacey? Apart from being sick? She's okay."

He stops himself. It's wrong to press the boy for information on Stacey Elder, especially information that may prove detrimental to her career. He asks if there are any questions about the battle of Jericho, or the wonderful tale of the Christian archeologists who proved that the story was true.

"No, sir."

"All right, then, go back to your reading."

By the end of the day he's exhausted. Deprived of his habitual afternoon nap Dr. Glaspie finds it hard not to be short with the freshmen in Stacey's class, who have spent the day confirming all her complaints about their demeanor. She has some real discipline problems to be dealt with, starting with Dale Canbury, whose comrades are just as bad; unkempt and sullen, snickering behind their hands at the lad's barely veiled cracks.

And their hair is too long. He considers once again the possibility of instituting, as is his right under state law, a dress and hair code, perhaps even requiring uniforms. The Catholic school in Gunnison has a uniform requirement, he knows, though only for the girls, and he vows to swallow his sectarian disapproval and ask Father Poplowski about how it's working out.

It's the hair, though, that really gets to him. Loath as he is to admit it, he feels a genuine, irrational dislike for the Canbury boy that is linked directly to that long hair of his. The boy looks like a hippie.

He remembers the revulsion he felt toward hippies in his

childhood, starting with an article in his parents' copy of *LOOK* magazine about the Summer of Love. At the age of nine or ten that revulsion metamorphosed into abject terror after the Tate/LaBianca murders, and for months he stayed awake as long as he could after bedtime, listening for the telltale scraping of tree branches and drug-induced giggling that would announce the arrival of the Manson Family, come to slaughter him and his family in their innocent sleep.

Though his fear abated, the revulsion and philosophical opposition remained. As an undergraduate he wrote a paper fiercely contradicting an instructor's quite serious suggestion that Jesus and the disciples were the first hippies and had to appeal his grade to the department chair when he flunked the course. In retrospect he understands that the instructor was young and foolish and not the emissary of Satan he once thought he'd identified, but the memory of that lecture still rankles. So, too, do those of the regularly occurring revivals of the style and ethos that kept cropping up over the decades, particularly in the days when Gower was still a tourist destination. Drugs and promiscuity were rampant in those days, and there are enough sad reminders like Darla Farrell around to strengthen his resolve.

No, the hippie movement won't take root again here, not while Edwin Glaspie, D.V.M., has a say in it. Newly invigorated, he sits at his desk and begins his lesson plan for the next day, postponing Stacey's indefinitely. Soon it's become a full-fledged lecture, not far in form or content from a sermon, and since only two members of the freshman class are Lutherans he can re-use it on Sunday. If Dale Canbury and his friends want to rebel, they will be made to understand that Jesus—despite some popular misconceptions suggesting the contrary—was no rebel.

He's already on his way out of the office when Gingie Bingham barges in and announces in her breathless way that Darla Farrell is very sick. A delightful gal, small and energetic, and a very good social worker, Gingie nonetheless takes everyone's word at face value, especially that of her clientele. This sometimes leads her to ask the impossible of her fellow public servants.

"Can you go see her?"

"What's the matter with her?"

"She's having trouble breathing."

"That's what she says when she wants attention, Ms. Bingham."

"She really sounds terrible."

He knows he has to go, on the off chance that Ms. Bingham is right; what he wants is for her to acknowledge his point that Darla Farrell is a congenital liar. But he knows she won't, and he ushers the woman out of the office without bothering to take his vet's bag.

Darla lives in what was once a storage space above the old Municipal Opera House, a handsome stone Victorian structure dating from the town's first brush with mineral riches and glory in the 1880s. Over the thirty years that she's lived there she claims to have heard and seen ghosts treading the boards below, arguing backstage and, most often, engaging in ectoplasmic lovemaking in what were once the dressing rooms. Not all of her ghosts are ancient; one she communes with regularly is the singer of a local band who died of a cocaine-induced heart attack onstage in the early nineties. She also claims to have been his lover while he was alive, the only detail in any of this that holds any water; Darla in those days was a sassy, good looking woman and prone to sleeping with anyone with a supply of cocaine or amphetamines, which back then in Gower meant just about everybody.

He lets himself in the front door with his Municipal Passkey and makes his way backstage in the dark. When Darla first lived here there was enough tourist trade in Gower for the Opera House to still see occasional use as a theatre, but after it closed the building went into a serious decline. When Buddy Gallego became mayor he put a stop to the city's longstanding efforts to evict her, something most likely to do with Buddy's history as an addict and Darla's encyclopedic knowledge of the recent history of criminal activity in the county.

Buddy is also responsible for the cleaning crew that comes in once a month, and for the exterminator's visits that have cleared out the ground squirrels, snakes, raccoons and various other wildlife that once scurried and rattled among the broken seats and dark rafters of the auditorium. None of the lights work, though, except the ones in Darla's space and those required by law on the stairs. Upon reaching the backstage stairwell he discovers that those are burnt out, and fifteen year bulbs at that. He pushes himself up the steps at a rapid clip, and when he raps his right knuckles on Darla's door he's pleased to note that he's not winded.

"It's open," she yells from behind the door.

He tries the knob and finds it locked. "No it's not, Darla."

He hears the sound but happily not the specifics of her cursing as she rises and limps across the room to let him in. "Hey, Eddie. Come on in and set your ass down."

No matter how many times he's called to the former storeroom he's always surprised at its neatness. Everything is in its place, there's no dust or grime, the dishes are always done. If you saw her here and only here and she never opened that freakish mouth of hers you'd think this was the dwelling of a nice old Christian lady. There aren't even any bottles around to bear witness to her prodigious thirst; she bags them as soon as they're empty to turn them in to Juan Stevens for the deposit. One windowless wall has been converted into a warren of shelves, all Darla's handiwork as far as he knows, laden with a lifetime's worth of music and movies and television shows, every one of them in extinct, unplayable formats. She has a phonograph and CD and videocassette players on a short table next to the shelving, but their power cords end in long-obsolete double prongs. She has no monitor screen, either; she may be the valley's only resident without one.

She's seated again, with her long, bony legs crossed at the knee in a way that would have troubled him deeply when he first knew her. Considering the rigorous abuse to which she submitted her body for so many decades she's in reasonably good health, but every hard day of her ninety or so years shows on her face and body. She scratches lightly at a scab the circumference of a half dollar on her left shin with a long, red fingernail. "How's the old horsecock hanging?"

By dint of will, he remains calm. "What's the problem, Darla?"

"Been having trouble breathing again."

"What kind of trouble?"

"I just told you. Trouble breathing."

"Shortness of breath? Congestion?"

"All that."

He takes her pulse, finds it acceptably slow. "You sound okay to me."

"You haven't listened to my chest."

"I didn't have time to get my bag at home."

"Yeah, you probably just wanted to put your ear right on my chest, right? By which I mean my bare chest? You guys are all alike. Anything to cop a feel."

"Tell you what, Darla, if you have anymore trouble breathing you call Chief Waxman, all right?"

"How do you expect me to call him when I got no phone?"

"Since when do you not have a phone?"

"Since I moved into the goddamn Opera House."

"Every dwelling in the county has to have a land line, Darla. There's a law. Now I'll get the town to pay for it, but you have to have one. That way you wouldn't have to wait for Gingie Bingham's visit to tell her to come get me."

"I don't have to wait for that dyke bitch to go get you."

"What did you call her?"

"Called her a dyke. Come on, you know it as well as I do."

"Darla, she's a very sweet young woman and I know no such thing. And you know as well as I do that that's a very serious accusation to be throwing around in the State of Colorado."

"Let her move her cuntmunching ass to California, then."

"I don't want to hear anymore of that kind of talk from you. Now until you get that phone you can just come get me if you need me. School or home."

"Liz doesn't want me over there at the house."

"Sure she does. Anyway it'd be a medical visit."

"Shit. Never thought the day'd come when I had to see a horse doctor."

"Neither did I, Darla, but that's the way things went."

Dinner is squirrel, a dish he disdained for many years, not out of any aversion to rodent flesh but because where he grew up in rural Missouri the people who ate them were poor and uneducated. His father, a small-town vet himself—many of these squirrel eaters were clients of his—used to mock them.

Now rodentia—rabbits and ground squirrels in addition to the gray squirrels—make up the chief source of protein in the valley, and he's come to prefer it to meats he used to favor, whose prices have long since relegated them to birthday and anniversary treats. His fear of his father's derision persisted for years after the old man had died, but finally faded; he feels some satisfaction in being able to imagine now, without shame, his father watching their dinner from heaven.

Dr. Glaspie takes a drink of his iced tea and sets it down. "I saw Darla today."

"How's she doing?" says Liz.

"Battier than ever. Does it seem to you like she's getting worse?"

His wife stops eating for a second, focuses on the farthest wall. "Her memory's getting weird. Not so much forgetting things as making things up. She keeps accusing me of taking Bruce

Ferguson away from her."

"Who's he?"

"Guy I used to go with. We drove to Denver once and saw a Foghat concert at Red Rocks. But this was '79, '80, maybe. You know, high school. Darla was a grown woman, married with kids. She never had any interest in him. But now she says she can't ever forgive me for stealing him away from her."

An image of Liz in her high school days with some high school kid in the back of his Falcon, spooning or petting or worse, springs unbidden to the forefront of his imagination. He banishes it, ashamed of himself. He knew when he married her that she'd had some sexual experience, more than he had, anyway; he's made it a point of honor for over half a century never to ask her for any specifics, and she has chosen to volunteer none.

"What am I going to do with her if she gets seriously impaired?" he wonders aloud. He breaks off a piece of bread and mops up the gravy from the squirrel, another uncouth practice forbidden in childhood that has become a habit in old age. "I guess what they're using now is Tefferin and Praxidane. I hate to think she may have to be sent to Colorado Springs eventually, but I cross the street to avoid her anymore. She accused Miss Bingham today of something awful."

"What?"

"I can't repeat it."

"What, said she was a lesbian?"

"She said the same thing to you?"

Liz laughs. She retains the charm of her youth, and he finds her very beautiful when she laughs. "You didn't know?"

"I didn't, and I still don't."

"Well, as long as she's discreet she won't be in any trouble."

"She will if Darla goes around calling her the word she used in my presence today. Remember what happened to that Russian hairdresser last year."

"Ivan was a little more flamboyant about it than Gingie is."

The land line trills and, having finished his plate first, he gets up to answer it.

"Dr. Glaspie? Chief Waxman here, I got an injured man here in the lockup and you'd better get here fast."

"What kind of injury?"

"Couple miners got into a fight at Consuela's, one of 'em pulled a gun."

"Then have the mine send their doctor."

"He won't leave the compound, says it's for insurance reasons. Company's backing him up, says we've got to release the prisoner to their custody, then their doctor can fix him up."

"All right."

The lockup still has more cells than have been needed for decades, and tonight is probably the first time in a year or more that a second cell has been in use. Waxman leads him back to the block to the holding cell where he finds an unconscious man on a cot, its thin mattress soaked through with blood, dripping onto the floor into a large viscous puddle. He takes the patient's wrist; the man's face is gray, his breathing raspy and thin, his pulse below forty. His shirt is gone, and the hole above his left nipple is bubbling with blood.

"I don't know what these boys were on, but I'm thinking probably Voltamine. Juan says they were laughing at something and then got real angry all of a sudden."

Glaspie doesn't know how that should affect the treatment, but he's out of his depth anyway. "It's hit his lung. You're going to have to turn him over to the mine. There's nothing I can do for him here, or even in the surgery."

"I'm not doing it. Those sons of bitches think they own this town."

"He's got a sucking chest wound and I'm a semi-retired veterinarian. If you don't have them send their ambulance over here he's dead."

"It's a question of jurisdiction. It sets a bad precedent."

"If you're afraid of what Buddy will say, I'll take responsibility for it."

"You can't take responsibility for it, Doc, you're not the police."

The loud, high, almost melodious sound of a siren comes from outside, disrupted every four or five bars by the jarring up-and-down diad of a klaxon. "I hope that's an ambulance and not an assault vehicle," he says, only half joking.

Two minutes later Chief Waxman returns with a man in a white suit.

"This is Dr. Glaspie," Waxman says.

"I'm Charlie Staller, with Lightnin' Queen Mining Company."

The man's head is almost perfectly round and bald with wisps of hair at the side and in front, like Charlie Brown's. His guileless eyes add to the impression, and Glaspie pictures him in a sweater with a zigzag pattern with that little beagle that walked on its hind legs.... Why is he thinking about the ancient comics page at a time like this? *Focus, Eddie, focus,* as Liz tells him ten times a day. *Focus on the man with the sucking chest wound.*

"What's the story on our patient here?" Staller asks.

"If you can get him a real doctor to operate he might survive. I can't do it."

"I thought you were the town doctor?"

"I'm the town vet."

"Jesus Christ on a pogo stick. Are you shitting me?"

"I'm not. I told the Chief here if he doesn't let you take him the man will die."

"All right. I don't want to start any trouble between the company and the town. How's about we agree to take him to the compound in your custody, Chief?"

Waxman nods and calls out to his assistant, one of only three other cops on the Gower force. "Marky, I'm taking prisoner Erno off campus. Write it up for me after you let those guys in the front door."

"His name's what?" the doctor asks.

"Erno. First name Laszlo."

"Other way around," Staller says. "Hungarian."

"He's a foreigner?"

"You got something against foreigners?" Staller asks.

"I just didn't know the mine was hiring any."

"Like it's any of your goddamn business who we hire."

"There's no need for that kind of language, Mr. Staller," he says quietly as the ambulance attendants from the mine compound rush in with a shiny new Chinese gurney. They load the man onto it, sticking him with an IV and mumbling to one another in an incomprehensible shorthand of acronyms and abbreviations that remind him, as if he needed reminding, that he's an animal doctor.

The next afternoon he's in the living room when he hears a keening sound in the distance, akin to a moose's mating bellow but many times louder.

Glaspie rises from his chair beaming. "And the truck is here."

"It's early," Liz says. "Shall we go ahead? Now if it hasn't been damaged in transit and if they got the color right for once we can get rid of this old thing." She picks at the back of the ratty teal sofa.

"You're always expecting the worst, Liz," he says, putting on his red gimme cap, despite her complaints that it makes his face look even pinker. "They very rarely make mistakes anymore."

She clucks her tongue. "You say that because you never have to deal with them yourself."

It's the biggest TarMart truck Gower has ever seen, a fourteen-axle model with auxiliary delivery shuttles clinging like parasites to the roofs of the trailers. A crowd of several hundred people has gathered to watch the unloading of the big truck and the dropoff and reloading of the shuttles, and they all listen in respectful silence as the captain of the delivery service barks into his loudspeaker.

"Anyone coming within fifteen feet of the truck or its crew will be dealt an electric shock that has caused cardiac arrest in some test subjects. If you have no hand-carries to pick up then we suggest you go home and wait for your goods to be delivered. If you have a hand-carry item your name will be called and you may approach Mr. Wilcox, he's the one standing by the Pickup Tent, and he will turn your purchase over to you. Lastly, if you have any problems with your purchase, now is the time to deal with it, since this is our next-to-last scheduled visit for this year. If you don't get it taken care of by our next visit you'll be out of luck because all items will be out of warranty by the time we get back in the spring, with the exception of large electronics."

There's a buzz in the air, despite the more than usually hostile captain. Downtown is as animated as it was on the Fourth, with small children running around chasing one another in the slowly diminishing heat of the early evening. People take out their cameras to record the offload and especially the dramatically noisy offloading of the delivery shuttles. Not far away, Bridget McCallum stands off by herself, ignoring the truck. She watches Cole talking to Neal Babb, who stares at her as if he's never seen an adult female before.

"What's that kid staring at me for?" she asks Glaspie without preamble or salutation.

He fights the resentment in his heart toward the boy but the resentment prevails. "He's just a bad seed. He looks at all the girls like that."

The boy flashes her a smug little Lothario's grin, complete with a salacious wink.

Cole expresses his disapproval by walking away, and when he reaches her, Bridget is ready to go. "Okay, shall we collect your stuff and get going?"

"What stuff?" Cole asks.

"From the TarMart truck."

"We didn't order anything this time."

She stares him straight in the eye to see if he's putting her on. "Why are we here, then?"

Cole is baffled by the question. "It's the TarMart truck. Gotta go see it."

"That's entertainment in Gower," Liz says as Glaspie turns to walk her home, arm in arm.

10

"WHATEVER POSSESSED YOU to think we should drive across the desert in July? Jesus, Buddy, have you lost your mind? The Sinclairs flew in."

"That's because you can't drive in from Rhode Island. It's impossible."

"And the Dengs flew in from Bakersfield. Don't tell me you can't drive from Sacramento to Santa Fe because I happen to know you can."

"I like riding in a car. You see more that way."

"See what? A whole bunch of empty desert in a hundred and fifteen degree heat?" Lena's right about that; the desert was an ugly ride, the only visual interest coming from the occasional rib-cage sticking up by the roadside. He closes his eyes and focuses on the rasp of her lungs forcing the air in and out rather than on his wife's shrill, strangled voice. "And how about me? I'm very, very uncomfortable, Buddy. My thighs are chafed raw and it's so fucking hot in here I'm about to pass out. And don't tell me to open a window because that's even hotter."

"Turn on a movie, why don't you."

"I don't want to watch a movie. I want to ride in an airplane instead of a shitty limo with shitty air conditioning. My God, you can't even manage to rent a functioning limo."

He tries to imagine a violent death for Lena that would have no political fallout. He ought to have guessed that ten days amidst the luxuries of Santa Fe would sharpen her sense of grievance.

The upside is that his daughter has spoken hardly a word since leaving Santa Fe. Greta is now obsessed with the idea of finishing her schooling at Señora Parker's Preparatory Academy for Young Women in Santa Fe before moving on to the New University of New Mexico. Buddy is all for her sudden interest in this decidedly worldly institution—anything to get her away from the Bible-shakers in Gower—but Lena rejects the idea out of hand as too expensive and too far away. It's jealousy, though, an inability to bear the thought of the girl reveling in modern city life while Lena languishes in what might as well be the 11th century. Maybe he should have behaved more like a Kommissar and restricted their access to the outside world; if they hadn't seen Paree, he might have kept them on the farm a while longer.

What cracks him up about it is that while Lena was getting her corns buffed off at the La Fonda with the other mayor's wives, he and Bill Deng took a guided tour of a couple of Santa Fe's worst neighborhoods, flyspecked Jebvilles of trashpickers rooting for microchips. In the vigilant company of half a dozen heavily armed sheriff's deputies they got a good look at the way three-quarters of Santa Fe's population actually live and die. No Big Grid for them, and no spa treatments, and that wall around the city center and the State Capital isn't there for show.

"Look," he says simply, "half the goddamn country's not on the Grid and those that are pay through the ass. You haven't got it so bad."

This sets off a torrent of new plaints from Lena and a surreptitious smirk from the driver, a Latvian refugee hired out of Denver. He'd smirk, too, Buddy thinks, having to spend two weeks driving Lena Gallego around and listening to her rant about the inadequacies of a luxury vacation that cost what the Latvian must make in a good year.

"If we'd flown we could have stayed at the La Fonda until this morning. Lisa Deng is still there right now. Probably getting a deep massage."

"You know what it costs to charter a plane for three people?"

"The city would have paid for it. All the other mayors got it taken care of."

"I have a little more regard for my constituents than some of those guys do."

He half expects her to laugh in his face at that one, but Lena is nothing if not proud to be the wife of a dedicated public servant, and she straightens her back. "All right. I understand that it's not the richest town in the west."

There was of course plenty in the travel budget to fly the three of them to the Conference. But stashed in coolant-protected cases in the underside luggage bin on the way to Santa Fe had been sixty bottles of Chateau Pétrus 2015 that had once belonged to a gay movie star and his pretend wife. The legal consequences for carrying booze onto an interstate flight, even as cargo, could be serious if he happened upon the wrong FAATFA man. And now those same cooler cases are filled with enough undocumented cash to ensure that any bribe would be ruinously lush. The conversion from yuan to dollars and the laundering of the cash is going to take a big chunk out of his profits as it is.

He saved one case of the stuff for Stacey; once he found out how much it was worth he figured this must be better even than their usual drink, and he figures she'll be so happy about the one case it'll never occur to her that there were five others. The buyer is, funnily enough, another gay movie star, Chinese, of course—the ludicrous prices the mainland oenophiles are willing to pay have driven the market for old wines beyond the reach of anyone else—and rich enough to afford a diplomatic passport that allows him to move the wine anywhere he cares to. Someday he'll tell Stacey what the bottles were worth, once they're all gone. He cares not at all about the wines themselves, but as he's sold off the Municipal Cellar over the years he's accrued a considerable amount of expertise on the market, and he's glad he doesn't have much taste for the stuff himself.

Another reason a charter flight was out of the question is the large and varied assortment of banned pharmaceuticals he picked up from Archie Stettle, the mayor of Tacoma. This is the real stuff, manufactured on the QT by Big Pharma, not the kind of trailer lab shit Rex Daggett peddles to the miners, and Buddy is quietly anticipating some intense new sensations in the coming weeks.

When they pull into the driveway of the Gallego residence Buddy has to get out of Lena's physical presence immediately. He tells the driver to put the bags away and pretends not to hear Lena demanding to know where he's going.

He's already wandered into town when he realizes too late that he should have taken a piss back at the house. The day's heat wafts upward into the night from the ancient, cracked asphalt of Fourth Street, and he sees nobody else out walking. Consuela's looks open, though, and he figures he can get a free beer or three off of Juan after he takes care of his business.

Once inside he cringes at the sight of Eddie and Liz Glaspie, waves at them and hurries to the bathroom, hoping Eddie won't come over and bother him, knowing that he will.

The thick, creaking spring, painted the same fiery orange as the walls, pulls the men's room door shut with a rusty twang and a thump. Buddy opens his fly and pees long and loud, wondering why he didn't feel the need on the road. For no reason that Buddy can imagine except to drive Eddie Glaspie crazy Juan has posted above the urinal a crude drawing of a topless and top-heavy cowgirl brandishing a pair of six-shooters, which Eddie keeps bringing up at City Council meetings on the grounds that it violates the town ordinance against aggressive or obscene public artwork.

The towel on the wall is sopping as per usual, Juan replacing it only every couple of days, and Buddy's hands are still wet when he steps out of the crapper. He takes a seat at the counter and Sal opens him a Coors without greeting him or asking what he wants.

"Evening, Sal."

"Evening, Buddy. You eating?"

He had a whole frozen pot pie in the limo, but on consideration he decides he might be able to force something down. "Burrito, please."

"Dinner or side?"

"Just a side."

"Side of burrito," she yells without turning to face the kitchen.

"How's Judd doing?"

"Lies around the house all day as usual. Wants me to fix him something to eat whenever I'm home, like he married me just so's he could have a waitress around the house."

"You ought to hit him over the head again."

"Don't think I ain't thought of it." She looks over his shoulder. "Uh-oh."

"Good evening, Mr. Mayor," says Eddie Glaspie, and Buddy can't bring himself to turn around and face him. He knows which look is on that pink face right now, looking for all the world like Santa Claus with a clean shave, like he's delighted to have run across *you* out of all the people in the world. This is the look Glaspie wears when he's about to tell you something you really, really do not want to hear. He knows without turning in her direction what Liz looks like right now, too: embarrassed and aggrieved, head probably in her hands. He sympathizes with the old girl, and when he's least inclined to cut Eddie any slack he usually does it anyway for her sake.

"Doc, before you say anything I don't want to hear I just

want to point out that I'm officially still off duty until tomorrow morning."

"I just wanted to see if Sal was regaling you with an account of the great excitement last week."

Sal takes a deep, allergic sniffle. "No, we was plotting to kill my old man."

Glaspie can't quite laugh at such a joke and he can't keep a completely straight face either; a shocked chortle and a disapproving scowl fight it out for control of his mouth. "We should probably discuss the shooting, Mr. Mayor."

"Will you cut out that Mr. Mayor shit, please? I've known you since I was ten years old."

"Dr. Glaspie here's shocked to hear the mine's been hiring foreigners, can you beat that with a stick?" Sal says. "Jesus, the guy who got shot's been coming in here for two, three years talking foreign and trying to grab my ass."

"Don't take the Savior's name in vain," Glaspie says.

"I'm not a member of your church and I can say anything I damn please. Right, Buddy?"

"Don't get me involved in this mess," he says. "Looks like my burrito's up."

Sal turns to get it, eyes still narrowed and trained on the doctor.

"Look," Buddy says. "We'll talk it over tomorrow, all right? Not first thing in the morning, because I have a lot going on right now."

Slumped over like a batter out Glaspie slinks back to his wife, and Buddy finishes his beer and starts in on the burrito as soon as Sal sets it in front of him. She gets him another beer without asking.

The rain is coming down warm and heavy when he gets home. The Latvian driver put the cases with the cash right where he told him to, in the cellar, and he doesn't bother checking to make sure it's all there. The White Stallion Limo Service was well remunerated for the trip.

He sits at his desk and powers up his screen, grabs a beer from the cooler and slugs it down, looks at some seasonal precipitation gobbledygook Glaspie forwarded. It's going to rain and snow like hell for the foreseeable future, is the gist of it, which isn't news to Buddy, and he kicks it off the screen. Back less than three hours and already the old man's driving him up a wall.

The trouble is Glaspie's no damn good at anything but being a veterinarian, and Gower has no use for one anymore. When Buddy was a kid, before anyone had even heard of cows with brains like Swiss cheese, there was ranchland all around, and three large animal vets worked full time in Gower alone, but the new, BSE-resistant breeds are so expensive no one around here's been able to afford to raise them, let alone eat them, in decades.

There's no more money to be made in sheep ranching, either, since the meat got so dangerous, and no one's flush enough to pay for veterinary care for dogs and cats, apart from the occasional bonesetting or euthanasia.

A few years ago Liz got him involved as a lay preacher at the Lutheran church just to kill his weekends—a ploy she surely regrets—but it's not enough to keep him busy, and neither are the human medical emergencies he's called on to handle. When Glaspie took over the high school a few years ago, Buddy thought he'd found a harmless way to keep the old buzzard out of his hair, but it isn't working. Karen Ingelblad makes the place function, really, and under Glaspie's regime scores have dipped so low that the district hasn't qualified for Federal funds in fifteen years.

He's rereading Chief Waxman's report on the shooting at Consuela's and finding it hard to follow when a tapping comes at the door. Lena sticks her head in the door and sniffs.

"How is she?"

Buddy's eyes are back on the page. "How's who?"

"You know goddamn well who. I can smell her on you."

"You smell Sal from Consuela's."

"You are disgusting."

"I didn't fuck her, I just went over for a burrito and a beer." He scans the page downward as if he's really reading the report.

"You ate in the limo."

"Have it your way."

"I suppose you're all for sending Greta to that school."

"Seems like a good idea, getting her away from here."

"If she goes someone else will marry *Neal Babb*." She whispers the name and looks over her shoulder, as though saying it might make it come true.

"So? He'll probably marry someone else anyway. And then who's left for Greta? Cole?"

"That'd work out nicely for you, wouldn't it?"

"It sure would," he says, but just to inflame her a little further;

in fact he doesn't really see what his angle would be in such an arrangement. Fond as he is of the lad he despairs of his turning out a normal adult male, and he's relieved, though somewhat ashamedly so, that Greta finds him repulsive.

"You keep treating him like a godson when his father robbed you blind."

"You don't know what you're talking about, Lena."

"He stole that desalinizer you had him working on, I know that much."

"You don't know shit. Now go to bed."

"I'll go to bed when I'm ready to."

For the first time Buddy looks up at her. "In any case," he says, keeping his voice low and even, "get the fuck out of here and let me read in peace."

He looks back down and waits a good minute before he finally hears her stamp away and slam the door. For a minute he indulges himself in a fantasy of strangling his old friend Ted Elder and burying him next to Lena, someplace dark and secret, and that cheers him up a little.

He highlights an article Jerry Doyle forwarded him as promised from Bloomfield Hills, Michigan, on interstate commercial rules for controlled substances in government custody, a subject dear to both their hearts. The conference was the first time they'd met, hitting it off on the first night when, after a long conversation about the lack of party loyalty these days, they realized that they weren't talking about the same party. In the end, they agreed that the important thing was to be a member in good standing of one or the other.

11

THE FIRST DAY BACK ON THE JOB is a predictable pain in the ass, with most of his energy given over to avoiding Glaspie and his newly minted nemesis, Charlie Staller of the Lightnin' Queen Mine. Charlie Staller, however, is used to finding people who want to avoid him, and at two-thirty he's seated across from Buddy, drinking a beer from the office cooler and wanting to know who the hell this doctor is who thinks the mine is any of his goddamn business.

"He's old and scared of immigrants," Buddy says. "He watches too much television."

"Here? How? You guys don't even get but two, three hours a day of it."

"You know what I mean. He takes it all at face value."

"Try and keep a lid on him," Staller says. "If it gets back to

Denver that we're having a problem with the locals I'm in the shit again. And that puts you in it right with me."

"How's your wounded man, anyway?"

"He's almost better. Your boy Waxman signed the custody transfer a couple days ago, so he's not your headache anymore. How was Santa Fe?"

"Hot and dry. Girls had fun."

"Speaking of rumors, I heard you did some business there."

Buddy's face freezes into place. "What business?"

"I guess you did," Staller says, and he stands up to go. "Hey, you know anything about some action over at the old Purdy mine?"

"No action there. It petered out when my grandfather was young."

"State Department of Biological Affairs put in a preemptory claim on all the acreage in that valley, we just got word from our man in the gov's office."

This sets Buddy's stomach rumbling. The land's worthless, if it weren't, somebody would have claimed it for their own years ago. But if it's worth something, he can't stand the idea of letting the state get hold of it.

After Staller comes Leo Elder, slapping a sheaf of papers onto his desk for later perusal. Something about him is off, something Buddy can't quite pinpoint.

"I don't suppose you ever contacted the governor about Lamar Collins's property."

Jesus.

Every burden he left behind is back on his shoulders the first morning home, like he never went for a vacation at all. "Nope. I will, though. Your Mom's all over me about it."

"No point now. They've left town."

"What do you mean left town?"

"I mean one day the girls didn't show up at school and neither did Gail, and when the Chief went to the house to check he found a note from Gail. *Gone away for a better life* was all it said."

"That's the most suspicious fucking thing I ever heard of. You think the Homeland boys picked 'em up?"

"I never heard of the Feds faking a note before," he says, "and I can't think what their angle would be if they did."

Right then Buddy finally puts his finger on what's wrong with Leo. "What happened to your moustache?"

"Got tired of having to pick food out of it all the time," Leo says on his way out the door.

After lunch he wanders over to the school and heads straight for Stacey's hut, its windows open perpendicular to the walls up and down both sides. He stands at the doorway and watches her lecturing the class about the heroic archeologists who found the remains of Noah's Ark and proved once again the literal truth of a Bible story. Knowing that she doesn't believe a word of it excites him; she's a bad lady, an adulteress and a multiple divorcée and a liar to boot, and it makes him crazy.

What kind of idiot stands around lusting after a woman he divorced twenty years ago?

The heat is starting to wear on him, though, and he knows she'll be pissed if he interrupts her in mid-lecture with some bullshit story about official business, so he wanders over to the office thinking maybe he can get this Eddie business out of the way.

Eddie's not there, but Gingie Bingham is, administering a test of some kind to Neal Babb. Probably some kind of psych exam; the Babb kid strikes him as a sociopath in the bud. Though he's unable to pin down the exact nature of this aversion, some intrinsic feature of young Babb's personality or physiognomy makes Buddy want to kick the shit out of him.

"Afternoon, Buddy," Neal says.

"Hello, Mr. Mayor," Miss Bingham says.

"Call me Buddy," he says to Miss Bingham, and, turning to Neal, "and you can call me Mr. Mayor, you little prick. Is Dr. Glaspie around?"

"He's at Darla's place. She's having trouble breathing again."

"I'll bet she is."

He sits down at Glaspie's desk and turns on his private screen, messes around with it until he finally gets onto a public channel and scrawl-scans Stacey a note.

```
WOULD LIKE TO SEE YOU THIS PM FOR SCHOOL/CITY
BUSINESS AT MY OFFICE.
B. GALLEGO
```

That done he returns to the office and awaits a reply.

In the street at six thirty he runs into little Cole Elder and the biologist, walking their bikes and speaking seriously and quietly to one another like lovers. She strikes him as good-looking in a way that he missed the first couple of times he saw her from afar, something about that slightly opened mouth with the prominent incisors, or maybe it's the slightly embarrassed and amused look in her eyes.

"Hey, Buddy," Cole says. "This is Bridget. Dr. McCallum."

"Sure, Stacey's friend. Welcome to Gower, Doc."

She holds out her hand. "Cole and I decided to have dinner in town tonight so Stacey could get her lesson plan finished," she says, then blushes and looks away.

Jesus. Even the stranger in town knows about him and Stacey. "That's good of you." Her long, graceful neck makes her look like a tall ballerina, and if he were seventeen he'd be stuck on her, too. She's one of those girls who radiate smartness, the way Stacey does. How, if he finds smart girls so arousing, did he end up with a dolt like Lena? Was she such a great lay back then? He doesn't remember, but that must have been it.

Cole and the biologist make their way towards Consuela's, the uneven dynamic between them almost funny; what's funnier is the fact that it's all down to an age difference of about ten years, and to Buddy right now she doesn't look all that much older than he does.

Stacey almost wept at the sight of the Pétrus '15, and sensing a big hit on his hands he failed to mention that he had the rest of a case still in the cellar. The Daggett Brothers' venison was superb, with a sauce Billy the Municipal Chef made from a jar of contraband blackcurrant jelly acquired from the mayor of Seattle. The sex afterward was just what he needed, particularly coming after a two-week layoff, and he's finding the segue into a discussion of school funding a difficult one.

"Can't we just lay here and talk about other stuff?"

"You told me you wanted to go over school business and I'm taking you at your word."

"Jesus. All right, go ahead."

"Look at what you spent on this dinner tonight."

"I hardly spent a goddamn nickel on it. The Daggetts gave me the meat because I helped their mother out with her landlord."

"What about the wine? My God, that was a lovely experience but do you know what a bottle like that goes for on the auction circuit these days? Go on, turn on your screen and look it up."

"I don't need to."

"You could finance the whole county school system for a year on that bottle."

"It's a small district, Stace."

"We need new equipment and a real school building. We need another teacher. Two more teachers. And whatever you're paying Glaspie it's too much."

"I hardly pay the son of a bitch anything."

"Still too much, Buddy." She sits up in bed, knees up in the air, and wraps her arms around them. "Are you listening to me? We need a real schoolhouse."

"New buildings are expensive."

"Says the man in the five thousand square-foot house."

"Three thousand eight hundred."

"Buddy, no one else in this town could even pay for the climate control on a house like that." She leans in close to him, a not unfriendly look in her eyes. "I'm just saying, with all you rake off the top in this town, maybe you could leave a little bit for the kids."

"It's throwing good money after bad." He winces; there are any number of good reasons not to have said that just now.

"What does that mean?"

He loves this woman, and in the moment he no longer feels able to lie to her. "Why build a schoolhouse when in ten years there won't be anybody living here?"

"I intend to be living here in ten years."

"You'll be damned lonely. The mine's about tapped out, the price of molybdenum's going all to shit anyway now that they're making tungsten damper fuses. What are people going to do for a living when the mining royalty runs out and they can't even supply the miners anymore? Shit, the mine doesn't need us, all that's just a municipal kickback. If the mining company doesn't spend a certain amount of money on local businesses they lose their claim."

"So really there's no reason for a town to be here at all?"

"Think back, Stace. When we were kids there was a tourist trade. Trucks coming through day and night, cars stopping in off the interstate. That little airport, even. Wildlife and fishing and all that shit. There were more than ten thousand people here, now it's less than two thousand. In a few years it'll be down to the Daggetts, living off whatever's left to hunt."

She digests the information slowly and unhappily. "What are we doing here, then?"

He puts his hands behind his head and looks into the corner of the ceiling and thinks about having the pressed tin restored.

Someone painted it over a long time ago, and an architecture professor from Boulder a couple of years ago explained to him a process by which it could be restored.

"What are we doing here," he says. "That's a good one."

"Just waiting to die?"

He holds his breath for a minute. "I like it here, and I'm planning to stay until the day I don't like it anymore."

"But you think that day is coming?" There's a plaintive quality to her voice, like she wants him to say it's not true, and he feels like just saying yeah, I'm kidding, it's great here in the glorious Rockies.

"What I think is you ought to liquidate everything you have and get ready to leave in the next few years," he says instead. "What's more I'd encourage your kids to do the same."

She gets halfway through a sentence that doesn't register on his brain at all because he's transfixed on the sound of someone outside the office, moving toward the door. Stacey seems unaware of the sounds until they culminate in the doorknob turning and the door swinging open.

"Jesus, Buddy, didn't you lock it?" she says before she even sees the intruder.

"Dear Lord, you've got a bed in here," Eddie Glaspie says in that strangled voice of his, looking like a boy who's just walked in on his parents.

"No shit," Buddy says. "Kitchen, too, and a shower. Sometimes I wonder why I ever go home."

Eddie's hands are in front of his mouth, and he looks mildly nauseous. "Fornicating on city property!"

"There's this quaint old custom of knocking on a door before you open it up," Buddy says.

"I see no need to knock when I'm here on City and School District business."

"What school business?" Stacey says, her voice higher in pitch than Buddy has heard it in years.

"You sent her an invitation on the school's mail system, from my desk, incidentally, inviting her to come over to your office and discuss school business. Well, sir, school business is my business."

"I got news for you, Eddie, there was no school business. I just wanted to get my rocks off."

Glaspie shakes his head, staring at the bed as though trying to decipher Aramaic, and points at Stacey, his face redder than Buddy has ever seen it. "You, Madam, may consider yourself on suspension for the time being until such time as a hearing can be held regarding your fitness to teach the youth of Gower."

Stacey's so mad she sits up and lets the sheet drop, and Buddy cackles at the sight of Glaspie swiveling away, his forearm in front of his face like Dracula confronted with a crucifix. "You son of a bitch, you had no business busting in here," she yells, bringing the sheet back up over her breasts. "I halfway think you wanted a look."

The sheer horror in Glaspie's eyes as they peek over his shirt-sleeve proves that this isn't the case, and Buddy stands up and puts his shorts on. "Calm down, both of you. Eddie, nobody's suspended, and there's going to be no hearing."

"That's for me to decide."

"All right, then. I can replace you tonight if I choose to do so. Now get out of here and we'll discuss what we have to discuss tomorrow."

Glaspie turns to leave. "I have never been so disappointed with anyone as I am with you two tonight."

After he closes the door Stacey starts laughing. "Disappointed, I'll bet. He knows goddamn well what we're up to." She puts on her brassiere and panties, slips her top on. He loves watching her dress almost as much as he loves the reversal of the process.

"What do you tell Lena when you're out these nights? That you're working on city business?"

"I don't tell her shit. She knows what I do."

"Suspects or knows?"

"Same thing." He shakes his pants, loses some change onto the carpet.

"I can't imagine letting my husband make love to me when I know he's sleeping with another woman."

"I don't fuck Lena anymore."

"Really?" She seems truly surprised. "You know what's funny? Right before Ted left we were doing it all the time. I thought things were pretty good."

She looks up at that elaborate ceiling as though she might see Ted there, then puts on her shorts and sandals and kisses him goodbye.

He takes her around to the rear exit, as if it made any difference, and watches her get on the bike and ride away.

Back at his desk he tries to watch a report about the corn crisis, but since he has no stake in agriculture it fails to hold his interest.

On one band there's another goddamned report on the First Lady's humanitarian efforts in Scandinavia, and he mutters a curse at Bill Scrope, the mayor of Hutchinson, Kansas, who told him last week a rumor that's ruined his many longstanding erotic fantasies about her. Scrope swears up and down that the President's better half is a fullbore post-op tranny with fully biogenerated female genitalia, that she was originally inserted in the President's inner circle by Homeland Security as a means of controlling him via blackmail.

Buddy knows this is absurd, paranoid stuff, but right now he can't help analyzing her jawline, finding it a bit too robust for comfort, her legendary bust a little too perfectly shaped, her supraorbital ridges a tad too thick. He knows he shouldn't have anything against trannies or regenerates but the idea has killed all the fun in the fantasy, and to put it out of mind he puts on a movie about a team of TarMart drivers who stumble onto and foil a subversive plot to poison the nation's supply of evaporated milk. He turns this off when he figures out who the villain is, a reedy kid with a crooked nose and a weak chin, identified early on as a draft dodger.

Hell, he was a draft dodger in his day. The lottery system wasn't reinstated until they were well into their twenties, and there wasn't much danger they'd be called up at that stage, but that was half the reason Buddy had married Stacey, who with her two dependant children qualified him in those lax days for an instant deferment. Ted Elder, on the other hand, volunteered and came home three years later with all limbs intact and a shitload of Tech Corps training.

That was neither the first nor the last time Ted made Buddy look bad, and Buddy's stomach starts to get sour thinking about the smart son of a bitch.

The anger he can still manage to call up over Ted's betrayal does a great deal to assuage his guilt over fucking his best friend's wife. Sometimes he thinks the guilt would go away completely if he told Stacey the truth, but it's too far down the line to start fessing up now to lies of omission.

Some satisfaction arrives in the morning in the form of Eddie Glaspie staring down at the pattern in Buddy's office carpet. "I'm very sorry for what happened last night."

"Liz told you to apologize."

"More or less, yes. I came home in a state of high dudgeon and once I'd expressed my disgust over your behavior she pointed out to me, quite rightly, that I should have suspected there was something untoward going on, and thusly should at least have knocked."

"You had to have figured out something was going on between her and me."

"I suppose I had my suspicions."

"Anyway, we got other sheep to herd."

"We do."

Eddie gets out his glasses and puts them on to read aloud from a stack of papers. "This is from the contract between the city of Gower and the county of Sloan, dated eleven years ago this month, regarding mineral rights, et cetera. In the matter of mine personnel..."

"I read it already, twice. Once eleven years ago and once this morning. I don't know why you've got such a bug up your ass about foreign miners. It's a shitty, dangerous job, why shouldn't they get some starving guy from Estonia to do it?"

"Those jobs didn't used to be nearly so dirty or dangerous. They used to be fit for Americans. Plenty of underemployed vets right here in Gower could use those jobs."

"And how many of them have all their limbs?" Buddy says. "Damned few. And there's not enough women who'll work around foreigners."

The appeal to the good doctor's xenophobia hits home and he powers down.

"Anyway the subject is closed. As long as the mine's paying the town its royalty and keeping us afloat I don't care if they're using slave labor or little children or the walking dead."

Glaspie frowns and plays with his glasses. "I suppose you're right. You going to services this weekend?"

"You know me better than that, Eddie."

"I only ask because I wondered if you and Lena might not benefit from talking to your pastor."

Buddy laughs out loud, and, filled with a sudden burst of affection for the old man, regrets hurting his feelings. "There's nothing to fix between me and Lena. Being the mayor's wife is a job to her, and she's pretty good at the parts that don't involve me directly."

Glaspie's disappointed in him again and in silence starts wiping his specs with his shirt. Why he didn't break down thirty years ago and get his eyes fixed like any normal person is a mystery to Buddy, but there's something comforting in watching him fog the lenses and then pinch them between the folds of his clean white shirt.

12

WHEN THE HEAT FINALLY BREAKS the temperature in the valley drops from the hundreds to the eighties overnight. A week later the highs are in the seventies, and at night it's getting cold enough for the leaves to start changing colors. Bridget remembers her grandfather in his dotage talking about fall in the Rockies, how he used to drive here with his second wife just to watch the trees turn red and yellow and orange. When she was little he used to tell her it was a shame he couldn't take her on a car trip somewhere fun—an activity she had a hard time imagining—and when he got really old he'd forget how things were and suggest to all and sundry that Wichita was getting too goddamn hot, and why didn't they pile into the car and drive to the mountains?

One September evening, the temperature in the forties and sinking, she heads into town by herself and stops into Consuela's for dinner. Seated at a corner table she looks up to see Juan Stevens leaning on the counter, looking in her direction, and winking for reasons unclear. As she's wondering why so many of the valley's he-men seem so taken with her, Sal breaks her train of thought by setting a bottle of beer down in front of her.

"That's from the boss. He says he wants you to feel like you're in your own place here," she says so joylessly that Bridget wonders if Sal doesn't pine for the old boy herself.

"Thanks," she says as Sal skids across the linoleum toward a table of Estonian lady miners who've been wolf-whistling at Juan. They'll never get him that way, Bridget thinks, not for more than a night, anyway.

Juan slides into the chair across from her, as graceful as any two-legged man she can think of. "And how's Bridget these days? Taking advantage of this fine autumn weather?"

"Sure happened fast," she says.

"Been happening that way for years. One minute it's a hundred and five in the shade, seventy percent humidity, then one night, *bam*, you're sleeping in your wool jammies." He takes a swig of his beer and furrows his brow, thinking hard. "Must be really cold up there at the lake. What, getting close to freezing overnight?"

"For the last week or so."

"You must be in like a triple thermal-d sleeping bag."

"Thermal-e."

"So, word is you're stepping around with Stacey's boy Leo. That true?"

"Not exactly," she says.

"You know why they kept him out of the Services?"

"Anxiety disorder, he told me."

He shakes his head, looks at her with his head angled as if he's trying to figure out what's the matter with her. "Can't picture you with a guy that age, especially one who's never been to war."

"Same age as me, like every guy I've ever been with."

Juan leans back, drapes his arm over the back of the chair. "Guy that age hasn't fucked enough."

"Excuse me?"

"To be any good at it." To her mortification, she starts laughing, but her laughter doesn't faze him.

"If you ever want to experience something considerably above average, maybe something extraordinary..."

"Juan, there's what, three women for every man in this valley?"

"So?"

"And half of the women who come in here are angling for you to take them to bed. Why are you so interested in me and Stacey?"

"'Cause you're the ones who keep turning me down." He grins and leaves the table, and she notices Sal staring from behind the counter, managing to make her face at once blank and baleful.

Bridget blinks and looks at the menu until Sal comes over to take her order. The fact that she even for a moment considered a roll with a legless sixty-year-old gives her pause, and taking a long swig of beer she wonders what the harm would be in a little casual sex with a more age-appropriate partner.

It's colder when she steps outside after her chiles rellenos, cold enough to make her zip her jacket up, and she walks briskly enough to get her heart rate up to ninety-two, according to her wrist display. She imagines her face will be flushed when she gets to the door from the cold and exertion, and she wishes she'd put some color into her lips before she headed out from camp.

Leo opens on the first knock and steps out onto his front porch. "Come in," he says after a moment's flustered hesitation.

The room is neater and homier than Bridget expected, a couple of big, ancient Arts and Crafts chairs facing one another across the living room, Navajo rugs on the floor and a painting on the wall of a group of Indians signed Berninghaus. She takes a long look at the painting, wondering if it's any good or not, whether she should express admiration.

"You like that?" he asks. "Got it from a confiscated ranch house. Some old time TV producer had a bunch of paintings of cowboys and Indians. I took most of it to the dump but this one I like. Have you eaten?"

"Just did, thanks."

"You want me to make you a cup of chicory?"

"Sure," she says, and she sits on the couch, a creaking, cream-colored thing upholstered with what seems to be real, very brittle leather, its spidery network of cracks repaired haphazardly with silver duct tape.

"I gotta get that thing redone sometime," he calls from the kitchen. "Came from the same house as the picture."

She hasn't had more than a mouthful of the chicory before he rolls the overhead lighting down and changes the tone to a warmer orange. Then he sits next to her and they leap into it in the frenzied, nearly panicky manner of the recently celibate, Leo wasting no time getting his hands inside her sweater. She surprises him by going straight for his belt, and he stands up.

"You know, the couch isn't great for this kind of thing."

"I guess not," she says, and he takes her by the hand and guides her off of the couch and into a bedroom. She's never seen a man's bedroom with the bed made, not when he wasn't expecting anyone to see it. They sit on it and neck for another minute, and then he stops again.

He goes into the bathroom while she sits on the bed, exhilarated and embarrassed by her zeal, which surprises her as much as him. He comes back with a small case from which he extracts a pair of syringes, then opens a tiny refrigerator and checks the dates on some medicine bottles.

"When was your last booster?"

"I don't know. Maybe a year and a half? Two?"

"You're not sure?" He says this with an exaggerated look of disbelief, as if he were a dentist and she a woman who didn't floss.

"I was in a monogamous relationship for the last two and a half years."

"But you're not anymore." He takes two bottles from the refrigerator and rummages in a dresser drawer until he finds a package of condoms.

"You really need one of those along with the shots?"

He shrugs. "You may have been monogamous the last couple of years, but I don't know if your boyfriend was."

"Right."

He prepares her hypo, drawing a measured amount of clear

fluid from the pink-labeled bottle. "You want to give it to your-self?"

She shakes her head. "You." She closes her eyes and does her best to relax her left biceps, and to her surprise feels a burning sting in her thigh instead. She starts, but he's a good shooter and the pain is momentary. As he wipes her skin with alcohol she rubs the phantom spot on her arm where she'd been expecting the jab. "Isn't it usually on the arm?"

"Thigh's better, with muscly arms like yours. Actually the buttock is best, particularly for women, but I didn't want to seem presumptuous."

He gives a placid smile and cleans his own thigh with a swab, then loads his own syringe from the baby-blue bottle, and within thirty seconds he's smoothing a square of adhesive latex on the spot.

"All right. We've got forty-five minutes to kill. Want to make out some more?"

An hour and a half later he steps out of the shower, having gallantly allowed her to go first, and pulls on his pants and a shirt. "You going to hang around for a while?" he asks.

"Probably ought to get going. I'm headed out to the Pit again in the morning to set up camp."

"Camping at the Pit? Like over by Purdy?"

"Yeah, I found some tadpoles in the pond next to it."

"Wow. I always wanted to go when I was a kid but it was strictly off-limits. Buddy and my Mom would have skinned me alive."

"It's pretty nasty. You can come see me if you want, I'll be camped a little further down the road so I won't have to smell it."

"I remember Ted taking Cole to see it a few years ago and my Mom was deadset against it. Didn't matter, though. Dad outranks stepmother in these cases."

"What happened to Cole's real Mom?"

He sits down in an old chair on the other side of the room that matches the living room couch right down to the crackling sound the leather makes as he settles. "She ran off when Cole was about four or five, couldn't stand it here anymore. Settled in Omaha, Nebraska and died that next winter of the dog flu."

"My math teacher died of the dog flu that year. So'd my dog."

"My Dad, too," he says, and she feels bad about mentioning the dog in context of all those dead people. She puts on her boots and sweater and stands. "I'll be back in town next week some time if you want to get together or something."

"Okay." He sounds neither horrified nor delighted by the prospect, which aligns nicely with her own feelings on the matter.

Her orders are to set up a new camp as near to the Pit as the air and soil readings suggest is safe, which is to say a good mile further down the mining road in the other direction. She'll return once a week through the end of the season for follow-up work on the freakishly normal amphibian life in Chouteau pond, whose surviving tadpoles have metamorphosed into adult frogs. With the first freeze they'll be burrowing under the frost line and she won't see them again until spring, with the exception of those she excavates for dissection.

She puts on her protective gear long before she gets to the

former town of Purdy, though it makes her breathing harder and the hike even more arduous, even now that the heat has broken. The Department has already offered her a well-funded expedition starting next spring, with assistants and new equipment and a piece of the action in case anything profitable comes from it. Coy about it so far, she's been as bold as to float the idea of a dual expedition under her leadership, with one team at Chouteau studying the normal frogs and a second canvassing the Pit with its myriad commercially viable possibilities.

There's been no word from Boulder yet but Bridget knows the pond is ecologically as important as the Pit, regardless of the variety of boner pills and weight-loss creams and wrinkle flatteners the latter might yield. She may try to hire Rex as a consultant, which may be tricky given his mistrust of officialdom, but she's determined that he share in any gain that may come from the Pit.

There's a dead raccoon in the sentry's post that wasn't there last week, and though the filter won't let her smell it she guesses it's been at least two or three days since it started attracting bugs and other agents of decomposition. It's the only mammal she's seen this close to the pit, with the exceptions of herself and Rex. She records its position and condition for her report and walks quickly to the pit.

On the bank of the pond she finds first one dead tadpole, then another, and then a third. Circling the shore she finds a dozen more, wizened and bereft on the mud. She kneels to examine one, nine or ten inches in length, its wrinkled belly translucent and stiff as the skin of a tomtom, its milky eyes dry and concave. There are no signs of metamorphosis in any of the corpses; she records their condition and numbers on camera and hazards aloud a tentative hypothesis: the drop in water temperature may be driving them aground in search of food or a hibernation spot, and their lack of adult limbs and breathing apparatus dooms them to suffocate on the mud.

There are still live tadpoles, sluggish and listless in the shallows among the sparse water plants. Bridget nets one and places it in a specimen bag full of preservative gel. The gel anesthetizes and kills the animal quickly and as she busies herself labeling the bag and putting it into her pack she hears a sound in the woods, coming from the dead trees to the north.

She puts her hand to the grizzly zapper, and through the splintering gray trunks spots an eight-point whitetail buck, his neck straight, head high, strikingly normal-looking. She grabs the camera and shoots, the deer staring at her for a moment before letting loose a throaty bellow that sounds to Bridget like a distress call.

Then it stumbles and collapses onto its front legs. With evident difficulty it rises again and turns in a disoriented circle before running off, crackling and thumping through the dried yellow and gray brush.

Bridget sets up the rudiments of camp a mile to the north in an even narrower part of the valley and surveys the area with dismay. She retests the soil and the air and despite respectable readings on both decides to take it two miles further out.

There's less than a month left before she returns to Boulder but three and a half weeks is a long time that close to a pitful of frothing biochemical mess.

The day's high—forty-seven—has already been reached by the time she rides into town with another Styrofoam cooler full of samples, including the only partially metamorphosed tadpole to show up so far among the hundreds observed so far at Purdy, its useless hind legs tiny and malformed.

There are several customers in front of her at the shuttle office, among them a woman attempting to return an unused, ten-year-old ticket to Casper, Wyoming and an elderly man trying to find out why the lady he's been corresponding with in San Antonio, Texas hasn't come to Gower yet, despite his having advanced her the money over six weeks ago.

When she finally makes it to the head of the line, though, Bridget's the only one in the place and, once her business is done, ends up talking to Bob for a few minutes.

He tells her the story of how he lost his eye, a jungle misadventure involving not Sri Lankan or Bengali insurgents but carelessness in a munitions warehouse involving an army buddy playing around with a Miniature Antipersonnel Device. Bob got the better of it, as it happened; the buddy went home *sans* arms, legs, eyes or external ears. His wife is after him to get one of those prosthetic eyes that move around in unison with the other eye, but he's reluctant to spend the money.

"VA coverage only provides a patch for my grade of service."

"Seriously? They won't even pay for a glass eye?"

"No, ma'am," he says. "Plus it being an accident and all, not a terror attack or a firefight, that puts me even lower on the priority list."

Outside it's so nice and cool that Bridget meanders around downtown for an hour, enjoying the presence of other human beings, even unknown, slightly batty rural ones; soon enough she'll be alone in the wilderness with nothing but monster amphibians and distressed ungulates for company. In the course of a half hour stroll she counts thirty-seven women and fourteen men and only three pre-pubescent children, school being in session that afternoon. Nine of the men are missing one or both legs, and one of the two-legged ones has a new-looking mechanical arm. One of the uninjured ones is Dr. Glaspie, who waves at her but hurries on his way without stopping. Fully seven of the women are missing at least one limb, a figure that surprises her.

Bridget stops at the old Opera House and admires its peeling facade. The lobby is coated with years of dust, and it must be full of whatever small mammals still subsist around here. Is this really where old Darla lives? She wants to get inside and take pictures of the lobby and the decrepit auditorium Stacey described to her, but the front door is locked. Seeing no other way to announce herself to anyone who might be inside, she knocks three times on the big glass pane set into the one front door that hasn't been boarded shut. No answer, so after a minute she raps again.

She steps back and sees the old woman crossing the dark foyer wearing an ancient white t-shirt that fits more tightly than Bridget would have recommended had she been consulted on the matter. Darla has on no pants or underwear, and her stiff white bush is wild and overgrown as a prospector's beard, in stark contrast to her luxuriant blonde mane.

"What do you want?" she yells. "This isn't a theater anymore."

"I wondered if I could come in and take some pictures of the building."

"I know you?" She's right up at the glass now, pressing her hands up to it to shade her eyes.

"We talked a while back, over by the Ghost Dance Gallery."

"That's been closed for years."

"I know, we were talking about John Whitefeather, how he wished he was an Indian."

"John's dead. All of that crew, dead for years." She turns back into the dark foyer and moves off on her dirty, heavily calloused bare feet.

13

TIME, PERHAPS, TO PUT PANTIES AND SHORTS ON and walk around town for a while. The dude who knocked on the front door sure did look surprised to see her snatch out there in the air like that. Wait, wasn't a dude, it was a lady.

DUDE look like a LAY-DAY.

What the fuck did she want to know about John Whitefeather for? Talk about your fucking methmouth speed casualties. Asshat's teeth were brown by the time he got put away, brown and stumpy and bleeding gums and all that other shit, just like on television. She never believed all that methmouth stuff, thought it was a big propaganda scam on the part of the government, until a guy she used to party with—was his name Lucky? if so, worst nickname ever—had a tooth fall out of his mouth once, right in front of her, gray and chipped and bloody.

Darla's proud of her teeth, even if they aren't her originals. They're still real teeth, and if they'd been able to regenerate teeth all those years ago well then that whole fucking generation wouldn't have started looking like hillbillies.

She puts on fresh panties and plucks a pair of shorts from its hanger. One thing they can't say about Darla Farrell is that she walks around naked outside her own house. Like she gives a shit about what they say anyway.

The soles of her flipflops are worn down to conform to the shape of her feet. Lovely feet they used to be. They had to be, her second husband had a very serious ladies' shoe fetish. The good part of that was that he'd buy her pretty much any kind of shoes she wanted, even real expensive ones from famous designers like whoever the fuck he was they were always talking about on that TV show. Chuck was a lawyer and made super good money, even for those days. The less good part was that once she'd worn them two or three times he started considering them his personal jizz jars, and four or five years into the thing he was fucking the shoes more regularly than he was her.

So. The flipflops. She wants to wear them outside while she can, because in a few weeks it's going to start being wafflestomper season again and she just fucking hates that. How's a dude supposed to look at a pretty lady's sexy feet when they're practically embalmed in about eight layers of wool and leather, laced up like a goddamn corset?

It's a long walk today, out on the old highway past where the tire store used to be. Too bad they tore it down, it was a pretty building in its day, with a big concrete whitewall out front. Squatters were living there for a few years, when that kind of shit was still put up with, and it eventually got so squalid even the crankheads didn't want to live there anymore.

Chief Waxman pulls over in the Muni Van and asks her if she wants a ride anywhere. "I'm just walking out to the edge of town."

"You're way past it now, Darla."

"I mean what used to be the edge of town, before." Jesus, she knew him when he was little Donny and now he's trying to boss her around. In those days his Mom Tinnie used to hang out with her afternoons at Mr. Bojangles and get hammered on margaritas and, later on when they got a little more sophisticated, some of your oakier chardonnays.

"You need water?"

"Got a liter bottle in my pack."

"Is it full?"

"Jesus fucking Christ, Donny." She pulls the bottle out of her pack.

"Okay, just making sure. I'll swing past later in case you want a ride back."

She waves him off. She can't dislike the kid but she wishes to fuck he'd let her alone. How old is he, anyway? Must be fifty anyway, maybe sixty, which means Tinnie would be, how old now if she was still kicking? As old as Darla anyway, which doesn't feel too old.

Steve Gilfoyle, that was Bojangle's name, had fucked Darla, too, come to think of it. The memory of the sex itself is long since faded into the vast wasteland of her erotic memory, its quality presumably somewhere on the spectrum between clit-bursting great and lie-there-trying-to-look-interested shitty. Anyway he's dead now.

The last outpost of the old outskirts is an abandoned Mobil station, its pumps still standing minus their hoses underneath the remnants of a canopy, the corroding tanks no doubt still leeching the last remnants of their petrochemical contents into the groundwater. The convenience store inside was a wondrous source of junk food and expensive trinkets, scratch tickets, and sugary frozen drinks dispensed from colorful, humming machines. She took the place for granted when it was open, was in fact a bit of a snob about shopping at the real grocery store in town and avoiding junk food, and now that it's gone she'd give a withered ovary to get it back. She dreams of the store regularly, dreams in which she's loading her arms with processed foods and carbonated drinks and foam cups of hot black coffee.

She sits for a while on the floor of the store and conjures the old place up in her mind, savors the taste of a Snickers in her mind, until she realizes what she's imagining so vividly is actually an Oh Henry! bar; the memory of what a Snickers tasted like is no longer accessible to her.

Back in town she stops at Consuela's and takes a table. It's five o'clock somewhere, she says out loud after ordering a beer, and Juan Stevens tells her it's well past five right there in Gower. In fact, it's almost six.

"Sun over the yardarm, is what we used to say. That's a sailing reference, Juan, you wouldn't get it."

"I get it," Juan says. It's slow, and he takes a seat across from her. "How's your day?"

"Some skank came by looking for me. I don't know what she wanted. Probably move me to Denver for medical experiments."

"They don't really do that, Darla."

"They sure do. Don't you read the papers?"

"The papers. Yeah, right after I listen to Fibber McGee on the wireless. Anyway that whole thing's an urban myth."

She takes a swig and realizes she's thirsty as hell. Then she remembers the water in her backpack, unopened. "Can I have a glass of water, Juan? On the house?"

"Everything's on the house for you, Darla." He goes to fetch the water and she watches his ass as he goes, marveling at those fake legs and how he navigates on them. Used to be that a man missing a leg was an unusual thing, even after a war, and they had trouble getting around, some of them.

When he brings the water she drains it and hands it back to him, then starts telling Juan about her and Tinnie fucking Mr. Bojangles, and Juan is real interested. Unfortunately at this instant she develops a sudden and urgent need. "Hold that thought, my back teeth are floating."

She gets up and waddles back to the bathroom, bloated and unsteady. Just for fun she goes into the men's room.

"You know," she says upon taking her seat again, "I don't really appreciate being confronted with demeaning representations of the female form when I go in to take a simple pee."

"Don't go into the men's next time, then."

"I believe I might like to have some french fries."

"I don't make french fries." He hands her a stained, wrinkled menu. "Anything on there, though, you can have."

When Darla gets home she stands at the bottom of the stairs leading to the apartment and sees a crack of light under the door. From her backpack she takes the electrical thing Buddy Gallego gave her last year without really teaching her how to use it, and she holds it in her right hand as she mounts the staircase. After a moment's breathless excitement she bursts through the door, brandishing the thing in front of her like Angie Dickinson and relishing the thought of killing some badass dude come for what's hers.

"Freeze, motherfucker! Hands where I can see 'em."

"Calm down, drama queen." Liz Glaspie sits on her couch, one leg daintily crossed over the other, a joint in her hand.

"Well that was just stupid. You could've gotten yourself killed, lady."

"Put that thing away. I told Buddy not to give it to you."

"What do you mean coming into my apartment without an invitation?"

She sits, and after a good long toke Liz hands the joint to her. Liz holds it in for eight or ten seconds before answering. "You *did* invite me. Plus you gave me a key last year."

"Huh." People used to tell Darla she looked like Angie Dickinson, which was a compliment even though she was so much younger than Angie. "What was his name, anyway? Guy who played her boss?" she asks Liz.

"Whose boss?"

"Angie's boss. Lieutenant Crowley."

"Darla, honey, you have to try and remember that I can't hear what's going on in your head. Who's Angie?"

"Dickinson. Who was the dude played her boss?"

"Oh." Liz takes another toke, blows it in its time toward the ceiling. "Earl something? Is that right?"

"He was pretty foxy for an old guy."

"I guess." Liz scrunches her face, wrinkling her forehead. "Holliman. Earl Holliman."

"He reminds me of your old man, kind of."

"Really?"

"He's kind of a douchebag sometimes, but I'd do him, if he wasn't your husband. Old Horsecock."

"Don't call him that to his face. That man devotes a lot of time and energy seeing to your well-being without so much as a *thank you* out of you."

Liz hardly ever gets cross with her, so she backs up. "Why don't you make him grow his hair back?"

"Eddie's one of those people who likes being old, Darla."

"Wow. I do not get that at all." She puffs again. "Kind of harsh to taste, but it's got a nice buzz, don't it? You know you ought to bake some of this into some brownies, mellow your old man out a little bit."

"Chocolate costs more money than dope."

"Buddy'd get you some, no charge. You're old town."

"Anyway he wouldn't know what hit him. He hasn't ever even had a drink of beer."

"I can't get him to prescribe me a goddamn allergy pill without getting an earful on the moral decline of the Rocky Mountain States."

"I know. He came home the other night just apoplectic because he'd caught Stacey Elder and Buddy Gallego in the act, right in the mayor's office. He said *Liz, do you know that man has installed a bed in the City Hall?*"

"Dope is the answer. I mean where was he when we were young and fucked up?"

"He was in the Air Force."

"Carpetbombing Charlie. That figures."

"He did no such thing, Darla. He missed that war by a good six or seven years."

"Really? I thought you guys were my age."

"Darla, I've known you my whole life. You've always been ten years older than me, and you always will be."

"Is he that young too? He can't be."

"He is, though."

This news genuinely takes her aback, the notion that the elderly doctor is a whole decade younger than she is. "You know half the time I talk to him he brings up abortion and half the time I think he knows."

"God, no," Liz says. "That'd kill him if he ever found out, seriously it would. Worse than if he caught me blowing dope with an old reprobate."

"And I say, Eddie, dude, abortion's fucking illegal in the state of Colorado, okay? You got what you wanted. And he says sure, but it's legal as close by as Illinois to the east and Nevada to the west, and we can't rest on our laurels."

Liz comes back to the couch and takes another hit. "I don't even hear it anymore. If he's a little nuts about religion and politics that's okay, because we live in a dying little town where it doesn't matter."

Darla's starting to zone out, and she leans back and wraps her forearms around the backs of her thighs and rolls backward onto the couch, sticking her calves into the air and kicking. "Check out my flip-flops, I just realized they don't match." She starts to sing, in what seems to her a remarkably clear and well-modulated voice:

"So step in my flip-flops, slip on a poptop..."

"Darla. Nobody wants to hear you sing, okay?" Liz barks. "Especially Jimmy fucking Buffett. That shit was old and tired even when we weren't."

"You know, I believe half the reason you come here is so you can cuss like that."

This sets Liz off on a laughing jag that builds until she's whooping and tears are running down her face, her left hand pressed between her breasts.

"And another thing, how come you never get busted for the smell?"

She catches her breath and slows down a bit. "Oh, that's easy. Eddie doesn't know what it smells like." Now they're both laughing, laughing like they're at a party or a restaurant in the old days when this was a real town and people knew how to party. The joint is down to nothing now, and Darla starts working on a new one.

"Oh, I've had more than enough, Darla. Don't."

She shakes her head. "I'm doing it 'cause I want some more, you don't enter into the decision. If you don't want it I'm not going to put a fuckin' gun to your head. Jesus."

"You know, after all these years I still don't like rolling my own. I never can seem to get it even."

"Yours are okay. It's not like there's a lot of call for it anymore."

Liz leans forward, her eyes wide. "We ought to make a bong, is what we ought to do."

"I betcha Buddy could get us a real one."

After Liz goes home she gets a little antsy and steps out again. She stops in front of City Hall and bangs on the door until Buddy comes into the foyer and lets her in. "Darla. How'd you know I was here?"

"You're here every damn night, Buddy. You can't stand going home is your problem."

"That's not true, Darla. I just got more work than I can handle. Been gone for two weeks."

"I got something I want to propose. Unless you got company back there."

"Come on in."

The office suite has a big picture of her first ex-husband Lance on the wall, and another of her daughter, Sudie. Both of them were mayor at different points, and neither of them lives here anymore. Lance doesn't live anywhere, strictly speaking. Sudie was only thirty when she was elected, but she married a fellow from China after just a year in office and abruptly moved there with him and started popping out babies. These kids don't speak English but they do send her friendly messages once in a while, machine translated, with pictures and video of themselves and of her tiny great-grandchildren, who to her eye don't have a speck of Darla left in them. This, she figures, is probably to their advantage.

"So what's got you out so late? You want something to eat or drink?"

"No thanks, I ate already and I'm fucking baked anyway. Hey, Buddy, I want you to get me a bong."

"You want me to what?"

"Get me a bong, you know, you fill it with water."

He leans back in his big padded swivel chair and puts his index finger to his temple. "Yeah, I remember what they are. Why do you want one?"

"Tired of rolling papers."

"Bong's going to get me into more trouble than the pot would if I got caught. If they catch me passing one on it's a Federal beef..." He shakes his head *no*, very slowly, his eyes open wide.

"It was Liz's idea. Smoke's harsh on her throat."

"Liz Glaspie? Jesus. You old broads."

She touches her hips and throws them from side to side like a bell ringing, flashing her most seductive smile. At least she thinks that's what she's flashing; her reconstructed lips are pretty numb after forty-odd years filled with collagen, twenty of those with Flaxopan, too. "Hey, Buddy, I heard you got a bed in here."

"Where'd you hear that?"

"Old Horsecock told me."

"Fucking Glaspie."

"You know, Buddy, maybe we could work off my pot bill in the sack. Where is it?" She looks around for something on the wall big enough to hide a Murphy bed.

"First of all, Darla, I get you that pot for free. Second of all, you know I'd love to give you a ride, and you know my wife doesn't care, but I'd have a hell of a time explaining it to my mistress." He winks. "And you know she'd know."

"I gotcha." It's been a while since she got it on, anyway, and she doesn't know how she feels about doing Buddy. But she misses the days when fucking was something casually done, partners selected whimsically and temporarily, consequences unconsidered.

14

IT TASTES AKIN TO SUSHI, only this raw fish is still on the bone, scales and all. It's a large brook trout, a foot and a half at least, the taste reminiscent of poached whitefish and very tender. Bridget takes another bite just below the second dorsal fin, ripping through the still-glistening skin and wincing at the mucusy mouthfeel. She's trying to think of a better way to describe the delicate, almost smoky flavor of the fish when it begins to move, or more precisely to struggle, as if on the end of a line.

In a panic she kneels and swings it by the tail against a broad flat rock, the way her Dad showed her as a child when they were going to keep a fish they'd caught for the family dinner. This fish won't die, though, and it keeps flailing desperately, with those two bites taken out of its side. It must be suffering terribly, she thinks as she strikes the rock again and again with the poor fish's head, the weak bones of its skull crunching rhythmically and wetly against the stone. The primary dorsal fin, spiny and slick, cuts her hands so badly she finally abandons the effort and drops the fish, whereupon she takes note of something hairy in her mouth. Looking down she sees not a brook trout but a cat, her old cat Mandy, howling in pain, with those two bites taken out of her flank, her fur bloody and torn out in patches.

She wakes, not screaming but inhaling a loud, sudden lungful of air, and she's torn between the dream and something wrong with reality. The air in her lungs is cold, and not Rocky Mountain-early-morning-summer or even autumn cold, either. She sits up, keeping the sleeping bag zipped, and pulls a warm shirt and a pair of sweatpants out of the bottom of the pack. She pulls them inside the bag and slips them on with some difficulty. Even the tiny amount of air that entered the bag during the process is biting cold, and she slips out of the bag and digs down further until she finds her coat.

It's not enough. Bridget puts on socks and her boots and sticks her head out of the flap. The sky is a flat gray with no gradations in tone, and the groundcover is thick with shining frost. She steps carefully outside and does a three-sixty. The frost dusts everything; her tent, the trees, the grass. It was forty-two degrees when she went to bed last night. Lousy goddamn Homeland Weather Service predicted a high of fifty today. She isn't caught entirely with her pants down, though, since fall always brings the possibility of early freezes and snow, and such cold weather gear as she brought will keep her reasonably warm even if the cold snap lasts the four or five days before her next scheduled trip back to the Elder ranch.

But the forty-minute hike to the pit is miserable, her feet blood-less and itchy in synthetic wool socks and stiff plastic boots, her knees stiff as Rex Daggett's and her face numb where the filter doesn't cover it.

She finds the pit frosted over at its outer edges with thin yel-lowish brown ice, with a big orange spot steaming in the center of it. The pond is completely frozen over, the beached tadpole corpses on the shore frozen solid. She spends the day dragging live ones from the bottom of the pond, their metabolic rates down to nothing, which raises the novel question of whether amphibian larvae of giant size can survive a frozen winter in a torpid state.

When she wakes, the light shining through the fabric of the tent is much brighter. Better prepared for waking in the cold this morning, she puts on her outerwear and once again sticks her head outside the flap.

There are at least six inches of snow on the ground. The sky is steely and cloudbound, more so than yesterday, and enormous downy flakes are still coming down. They fall not in the leisurely manner of big fluffy snow back in Kansas, though, or even in Boulder; this is snow in a hurry to accumulate and prevent her return to civilization. It's so quiet she can hear the flakes landing, until a crow shrieks, echoing out across the snow and against the frozen mountains that surround her.

Today the hike takes an hour and a half. The snow is already kneedeep in spots, and her breath is ragged and painful when she reaches the pit. She's surprised to see that its center is still liquid, though the dirty ice around the shore has inched further inward and thickened. The ice on the pond is already three inches thick in spots, and she wonders whether her work is done for the season.

In the sky coming in from just past the peaks to the north she's thrilled to spot a *V* of Canada geese, the first she's seen since her childhood. It's a small group, nine or ten birds in ragged formation, and once they spot the liquid water of the pit below they begin a frantic descent punctuated by ugly honking. She waves her arms frantically at them, yells, steps into the snow agonizingly slowly until she reaches the pit, where she paces back and forth across the north shore, trying to frighten them off. They fail to change course, and to her horror she sees the lead bird heading for the center of the pit, where it sets down, followed one by one by its flockmates. The honking continues and she thinks she can hear a new note in it, one of terror and revulsion, as the birds that have landed flap and struggle to get out onto the ice, which leaves room for other birds to take their turn. Not a minute has passed before the first bird is sprawled steaming and dead on the dirty ice, and in five the entire flock is dead or dying in the chemical soup, on the shore, or on the ice.

Upon her disheartened return to camp early in the afternoon she hears a double grunt not unlike that of a man clearing his throat to announce his presence. It's an animal sound, though, something huge, and Bridget grips her bear zapper, hoping to God it's not a bull elk or, God forbid, an actual bear looking for a pre-hibernation protein supplement. She's not even sure bears still live here, or that her zapper is charged.

Bridget peers around the corner of the tent. Rex Daggett sits in her folding chair, serene and kingly, a big canvas bag next to him. He nods at her and grunts again, and even seeing him do it she finds it hard to believe that the sound comes from a human.

"Miss McCallum."

"Hi, Rex."

"Early snow."

"Yeah, so I noticed."

"Thought I'd bring you something to eat."

"Thanks."

He opens the bag and she looks inside. It's a couple of kilos of raw meat, vacuum sealed. "Venison," he says. He snorts, and she can hear a load of snot traveling through his sinuses before he spits it into the snow. "Sure hope you're not planning to pass the winter here."

"Just the next couple of weeks, then I'm going back to Boulder."

"How?"

She's about to say *on my bike* when she realizes how stupid that would be. "I guess I might have to spend the winter in Gower."

He nods and looks away. "If you can get to Gower."

"Do you think I might need some kind of vehicle to get back to the county road?"

Rex extends his lower lip in a thoughtful pout and grunts. "Don't see how a vehicle'd be of much use one way or the other. Ice axe, maybe. But if you wait too much longer you'll be up here all winter."

"Just a day or two more while I wrap up the work."

He doesn't nod, just looks away into the distance.

"I have to take more water samples before I go, and I have to figure out how the tadpoles are managing to hibernate."

Still not looking at her he takes a deep breath with his mouth closed. "Thought those people were real happy with what you were doing up at Chouteau."

"They were, they're just more interested in this. I'm going to try and study both next year, if I can get enough leverage out of this one."

"They're real interested in whatever's doing this, ain't they?"

"They are," she says, feeling as if she's admitting to something.

"Thought that might happen. Been finding a lot of animals around here with things wrong the last couple, three years. When I seen them gollywogs I figured it was something in the pond. Just got clear enough to drink a few years back. Not that I ever would have, but an elk doesn't know better."

"You never know what you're going to find in a soup like that that's been left to fester for eighty or ninety years. Bacteria and biochemical compounds no one's ever thought about."

"Which is good for what?"

"Making new medicines, for one thing."

"Like boner creams and footstink powders, huh?"

"Or cures for cancers or neurological diseases or the flu."

"*Cure cancer*," he says, and his level gaze makes her feel caught in a lie. "Or maybe some kind of new poison for the Armed Forces, you think?"

She nods. "I guess there's a chance of that."

"Anyway, you see that you're out of here next couple days, because after that it'll be too late to get anywhere, and I don't aim to feed you all winter."

15

HE ARRIVED IN DURANGO YESTERDAY via the Santa Fe shuttle, intending to take the next morning's Gower shuttle. The afternoon was breezy, the September cool-down several weeks early, and he was almost looking forward to the next day's arduous trip.

Durango didn't used to be much compared with Gower or Aspen, but it's lost less of its tourist town charm than Gower has, and less of its population. There's a well-maintained if poorly traveled road going through it still and the locals are out in force on the sidewalks and streets. The bicycles look new, most of them, if not as new or fancy as the ones on the streets of Hong Kong. In his time in China, he's become used to the presence of cars again and it seems odd being back where they're rare, save for the occasional Municipal Van or TarMart truck.

The first evening he went out for dinner and treated himself to a real steak instead of venison, washed down with cold, flavorless Colorado beer, and paid for the meal in cash. His waitress, twenty or so and possessed of a guileless, happy smirk and wearing a distractingly tight-fitting top, flirted with him when she brought the bill.

"Ted," he said when she asked his name. "I work in China."

"*Ooh,* I learned some Chinese in high school but not enough. I'm going to take some night classes, though. I'll get there some day." She looked to be of Ute origin, and though he understood her desire to leave he wished she could appreciate the simple glory of a town with a little bit of life left in it, the kind that still surfaced when he dreamt of *home*. If he'd been in any position to stay in Colorado, he would have chosen to stay here.

He went to bed that night in a plush corner room on the third floor of Durango's oldest surviving hotel after watching a century-old black and white movie on the room's big but fading screen, a preposterous western about a crooked sheriff and a family of killers on the prairie. Around three he awoke and got a glass of water from the tap—a real old-fashioned bathroom tap with no filtration, like you still saw in these tiny burgs and nowhere else—and found the room unusually cold, but didn't bother to look out the window before climbing exhausted back under the covers.

Now it's morning and he's sitting in the hotel lobby drinking coffee, which the white-haired, gray-toothed waiter tried to dissuade him from ordering, presumably because Ted doesn't look like the sort of person who could pay for real coffee. He ordered a small pitcher of milk on the side, although he loathes the stuff, just to make a point. Setting it on the table the waiter pointed out that this was real cow's milk from a small artisanal dairy farm in Ouray and not that Christawful horse cream you get most places.

Ted doesn't care, couldn't tell horse's milk from cow's from elephant's if he saw it streaming from the teat. He's halfway between enjoying the hot coffee and despairing at the sight of the thick white stuff outside the window, coating the sidewalks and the streets. A snowmover crawls down the street outside pointlessly; this is the kind of snow that keeps piling on for days, and no matter how much you get rid of the place never gets navigable, never becomes functional until the snow stops. Then you can get rid of it for a day or two, before it starts again.

Of course, he could be wrong. He's never seen a snow this heavy this early in the year, not this low, maybe a few phantom flakes that vanished upon contact. The waiter told him when he came down that all shuttles are canceled until further notice, which might mean for a day or two if this is a freak thing, or might mean until spring, if this is the kind of evil tempest it looks like from where he sits. A long stay in Colorado isn't something Hong Kong Desalinization Ltd. will allow him—it was difficult enough getting them to agree to his coming back at all. Pondering his options, Ted's mood sinks.

When he's finished with the coffee he tramps through the drifts, already up to his knees in spots, to the shuttle office. While he waits in line he hears the young woman in charge tell the same story to five different people, all of whom wait patiently, and none of whom dare challenge the authority of her bright green shuttle uniform. Why would you wait in line listening to the same question asked again and again if you didn't intend to try and get a different response, he wonders, but they don't. The woman is six feet tall at least, gawky and pretty, the sides of her head shaved in a manner fashionable among urban sophisticates five or six years ago. Her unsteady gaze reveals a profound discomfort in her position of authority.

"I'm wondering about the eleven o'clock shuttle to Gower," Ted says when his turn comes.

"That's the eleven-oh-seven to Boulder?"

"If that's the one that stops in Gower."

"It's canceled until further notice."

"Why is it canceled?"

She looks like it's the first time all day she's been tempted to laugh, and she goes ahead and lets one out, pointing out the picture window at the dreary, blindingly bright scene outside the window. "It's snowing like crazy."

"Not bad enough to stop a shuttle with weather gear. It'd have to snow a couple more days before they'd really be in trouble."

She seems happy for the diversion of an argumentative customer. "Mister, you're absolutely right. It's just company policy, if it snows more than six inches we put the brakes on until it melts."

"So there's not a single shuttle likely to leave here until the next melt?"

"Nuh-uh."

"How about a refund?"

"I'm not authorized to hand you one, but if you can wait until the regional supervisor gets in he can get you one."

"How come he's not here? Seems like this is a moment of crisis."

She scratches her nose, her nails long and enameled a brilliant orange that matches her lip gloss. "Well, he's on his way from Boulder."

"On a shuttle."

"Yeah. Kind of."

"So he's very unlikely to get here at all before, say, May or June."

"Um, the message I got an hour ago was that he was on his way."

Ted sincerely wishes her a pleasanter morning than she's been having and leaves. He doesn't care about the refund—it's Chinese money anyway, lots more where that came from—but he has to get to Gower, so now he has to get creative.

If you need something illicit in a strange town, you ask the bellhop. This was a pearl of wisdom Ted's grandfather had given him in his childhood. Reluctant as he is to put into practice what he has long treasured as the single most useless piece of advice ever, he's desperate, so he wanders the corridors until he corners the bellman on the second floor. Easily as old as the waiter in the restaurant, he bristles when Ted asks him if he knows where a man could get a ride out of town during a blizzard.

"Man would have to have a whole shitload of money." The bellhop's gray-and-yellow handlebar moustache bristles as he moves his jaw from side to side as if to loosen it up.

"Okay, say this man's got a whole shitload of money."

The bellhop gives him a scathing once-over not far in spirit from the one the waiter did earlier, and Ted feels compelled to pull out a large bill. Even if Durango's service economy is functioning at a level twice as high as Gower's this is probably twice what the old man makes in a week, and he scoops it out of Ted's hand and it disappears into his pocket. "You ought to buy yourself a new suit of clothes, man."

"I've been on the road. So tell me where I can get a ride north."

"North is a big direction. Canada? Michigan?"

"Just as far as Gower."

"That's good. There's a Federal prison convoy heading out in two days for Colorado Springs. Those Correctional Corps guys get where they're going no matter what. Sixty inch wheelbase. Driver's name is Slavko."

"First name or last?"

"Who gives a shit? He's from Latvia or Poland or some other place that's not a country anymore. Main thing is, if the driver's a big black dude, name of Larry, you turn around and walk away 'cause Larry's strictly by the book. In fact if you try and get on his convoy you might just end up in the jug yourself, *capeesh?*"

"Got it," Ted says.

"You go out to Mandy's Chicory Hut, that's two blocks over, Slavko ought to be there. He's headed today for the Federal lockup in Gallup and he'll be back from there in a couple days with a shipment for Colorado Springs."

In two days, he thinks, the shuttle might be running again, but it's good to have a fallback position.

Over the next forty-eight hours the snowfall never lets up for more than an hour or two and by the time he shows up to rendezvous with Slavko, Ted has begun to worry that even the hardy men of the Federal Penitentiary Service might be tempted to back out of this trip. Slavko is waiting for him, though, at the Federal Vehicle Management Administration hangar on the far east end of town and slaps Ted on the back when he hands over three thermoses full of hot black coffee and a smaller one of real artisanal milk from the hotel.

"Haven't had a drop of the real stuff in ages," Slavko says. Thirty or so, with a long, curly beard like an Orthodox bishop's, he sounds just like the late King of England. "Chicory and Noxadrene hasn't quite the same effect on a long drive, has it?"

The vehicle is lowslung and immense, with a long windowless trailer, its gigantic tires treaded inches deep for traction in snow and mud. Slavko climbs aboard the cab and beckons. "You'll keep out of sight until we're on the road, then you can come back up front." Ted squeezes into the sleeping compartment behind the cab and closes the partition.

A few minutes pass before the door to the cab opens again and a man in a government jumpsuit clumps in on his wafflestompers and then opens the partition for a look. "Howdy," he says.

"Hey," Ted says back.

"Hear you're coming with." The man has all his limbs and external sensory organs intact but his scalp is massively scarred, with just a day or two's worth of blond fuzz where it isn't.

"Heading for Gower."

"Let you off at old State 63, then, is probably closest."

"There's a road ten miles further that leads to a molybdenum mine. It's going to be quicker that way on foot."

"Man, that's a great way to get your ass shot off, walking through mine company property." He extends his hand. "I'm Steve. Licensed Vehicle Operator."

"Ted."

"Slavko says you're paying in yuan."

"Yep."

Steve laughs and slaps the bulkhead. "I'll take it when I can get it, man," he says, then climbs back over into the cab, where he and Slavko go over various checklists in preparation for departure.

Ted wakes up with the feeling that he's on horseback, but as he orients himself he thinks it's more like riding a horse underwater, smooth and undulating. He sticks his head through the partition cautiously, unsure of whether he's allowed to come out yet.

"Look who's up," Steve says, his unbooted feet up on the instrument panel. "Come on in and sit."

"Where are we?"

"We're just about thirty clicks out."

"Making excellent time," Slavko says.

"Okay for snow, anyway," Steve says.

"How'd Homeland Weather get this so wrong?" Ted asks, taking the third seat. "Even with a freak thing like this you'd think they'd have had some clue it was coming."

Slavko and Steve both start laughing. "Homeland Weather Service, shit," Steve says.

"They knew all about it, they just can't admit that their twenty-one day forecast is wrong, so they won't alter it more than slightly as the day in question approaches. Usually they're quite close to the mark, so it's not a problem. But we in government service don't rely on them at all." Slavko takes a big drink from one of the thermoses.

"The government doesn't use its own weather service?"

"Ssshh. There's a joint Sino-Indian service called Meteo-Logic."

Steve says, "But part of the deal is they'd have to say that they were using it. Well, you think the U.S. government is going to admit that a bunch of foreigners can do something better than they can?"

"Wish I'd known about that."

"So are we to presume that you are in the employ of the Chinese?"

"Sort of. I'm on a temporary leave of absence. What are you guys hauling, anyway?"

Slavko lowers his voice to a hoarse stage whisper. "Prisoners, Ted."

Steve leans over toward Ted with his hand cupped beside his mouth. "That's a big secret. Not supposed to ever, ever acknowledge prisoner transport. So keep your mouth shut."

Ted nods.

"Don't be melodramatic, Steve."

"*Mellow dramatic,*'" Steve drips in a pretty decent impression of Slavko's accent. "This cocksucker wants everyone to think he's a limey, but ain't, he's nothing but a fucking russky."

"I don't want anyone to think any such thing, Steve. For one thing the name Slavko's a dead giveaway, isn't it? Wouldn't I change that if I wanted to be taken for English?" He turns to address Ted. "Brought up in Moscow, in the good old days of oligarchy and excess. Pee and Emm hired an English couple as nanny and tutor." He goes quiet and watches the road and the monitor, manipulating the steering column with a light touch.

A low tone starts blaring from the speakers, which both Steve and Slavko ignore. "What I don't get," Steve says, "is how this fucking foreigner rates a government job as an LVO. I'm thirty-six years old and damn near got my head blown off my neck serving my country and it still took me five years on a waiting list before I got taken on."

"I have a master's degree in Administration of Justice," Slavko says to Ted. "Steve's got a high school equivalency degree from the Veteran's Rehabilitation Administration."

"Yeah, so driving a truck's not good enough for this asshole," Steve says, hands locked behind his head. "Wishes he was a warden someplace."

"When I am I'll make you my administrative assistant."

"Like I'd take orders from a eggheaded fake limey shitbird russky." Steve laughs, mouth lined with perfectly straight, brilliantly white regenerates.

"What's that buzzer?" Ted finally asks.

"That's one of the guards wanting something. Don't worry, if it's serious they'll hit code three. That's a code one right there."

"Violent insurrection is code six. I never respond to less than a code four," Slavko says, stroking the beard just below the chin.

"Answer them every time they buzz and they'll abuse the privilege."

"I wouldn't worry about any code six from these guys," Steve says. "This is a blue shipment, which means only gimps and nonviolent offenders, and we take the gimps' peglegs away before we load 'em up."

"We're headed for Colorado Springs," Slavko says. "Which almost certainly indicates a shipment of subversives."

Steve perks up. "Speaking of which. You want to have a little fun?"

Slavko, dubious, looks over at Ted with his upper lip curled. "Not something our guest necessarily wants to participate in, Steve."

"Come on. I don't want to have to wait until after we drop him off. Besides it'll be more fun with a third guy." He looks Ted in the eye. "Do you double fucking pinky promise me you can keep a secret?"

Sketchy though this sounds, his need to stay on their good side trumps his sense of dread. "You're taking a risk for me, I can keep quiet about anything you want."

Steve looks like a bright-eyed kid on Halloween holding a bag of dogshit and a match. "Stop the truck, Slav."

Slavko hesitates, then he looks over at Ted and grins. He applies the brake, and the truck slows to a stop.

"Now here's the deal. We been super careful these assholes didn't get a look at Slavko. Only guy they've seen is me." He presses a button on the dash, which illuminates a ghostly green, and removes two automatic weapons from the armory in the sleeping deck behind the cab, handing one to Slavko and the other to Ted. Then he opens the passenger side door and the three of them descend into the snowbank.

Slavko pounds on the cargo hatch at the rear of the truck with the butt of his rifle.

"Who is it?" says a voice from the door-mounted speaker.

"Steve. Everything's copacetic. Open up." He winks at Ted, whose general nervousness is not allayed by the sight of Slavko sticking the barrel of his weapon against Steve's temple. "Look like a badass terrorist motherfucker when that door opens," he hisses at Ted, who is starting to worry that this may be an elaborate plan to kill him.

When the door opens Steve looks terrified, actual tears pooling in his lower eyelids. "Jesus Christ, Jorge, do whatever the fuck they say."

"All right, listen tight," Slavko says, his accent suddenly very convincingly Slavic. "All prisoners is free. Guards don't make any fuckups and they live, othewise it's dead time. Is liberation camp for American prisoners one click east of here. Put on prosthetic legs if you needs to and run like motherfuck through the woods. You," he says to the guard, a nonplussed blond giant presumably named Jorge, "get their legs out of case."

Steve is blubbering by this point, begging Slavko for his life with admirable actorly restraint and not allowing his voice to crack more than absolutely necessary. Jorge and the other guard unshackle the prisoners and help them replace their artificial legs—at least two thirds of them are single or double amputees, their replacement legs mostly out-of-date military issue—and push them out into the snow. One, a flatfaced, burly old man with thatchy white hair and a pair of perfectly round, surgically sculpted holes where his nose used to be, looks straight into Ted's eyes and conveys wordlessly though nonetheless eloquently a desire to tear his fucking lungs out by the bronchia.

"All right," Slavko calls into the darkening gray sky. "Fall in, boys." Like the soldiers they almost certainly all once were they line up, some at a better imitation of attention than others, and the big Russian paces before them, leaning forward slightly, hands joined behind his back. "Here is drill. One click east through snowy woods. Food and camp and passage to overseas. *Go.*"

Two brave souls break off towards the aspen, taking high dainty steps through the drifts and making very bad time in their rush to freedom. Though this is exactly what Ted imagined would happen, the worst hasn't come yet, and he tries and fails to believe that it won't. His impulse is to drill one straight through Slavko's skull, following him up with Jorge and the other guard before killing unarmed Steve, but whatever animal instinct kept him alive twenty years ago in the rainforest tells him now that his weapon is unloaded, that he's merely a dress extra and not to be trusted with live ammo.

The prisoners shiver, dressed for a warm truck ride and not games in blizzard conditions, casting sidelong looks at one another. Some of them shrug, others give terse little negative shakes of the head. "*Go, go!*" Slavko yells, and three more men take off, then another three, and another four, despite the quiet efforts of some of their fellows to restrain them. The ones with the government-issue prosthetics are having a better time of it than the others, leaping with ease in and out of the crotch-deep banks. "Is that all the men brave enough to join resistance force?"

The faces of the remaining men are blank, awaiting nothing more than the order to return to the truck.

"All right, then," Slavko yells, voice plummy British and jolly once again, and he turns and fires on one of the lead runners. Slammed in mid-leap, the body does a half-twist and falls forward, disappears completely into the snowbank just as the man next to him goes down. Steve has pulled a semi-automatic sidearm and fires happily, letting out little whoops when he hits a runner. Jorge and the other guard watch with the mildest of amusement, looking annoyed at the delay as they remove the prosthetics from the remaining prisoners, face-down on the ground and hyperventilating, some of them crying. At least one of them has shit himself.

Ted looks up and notices that the shots have stopped. Slavko and Steve are laughing so hard they have to lean against the truck to stay upright. "You should have popped a couple," Steve says, catching his breath.

"Isn't loaded," Ted says.

"Dumb shit, you got the safety on." Steve takes the weapon from Ted and fires it down into the nearest of the dead, the impact pushing him further into the snow.

"I tell you what, those fuckers were fast, considering."

"What do you do with the bodies?" Ted asks.

"Standard operating procedure on a code six is leave 'em there for the crows." Jorge and the other, nameless guard are herding the remaining prisoners onto the truck with a chairlift. One of them is breathing ragged and wet, between the excitement and the cold and his barely controlled weeping. "Don't worry about 'em. You got to cull the fast ones, they're always trouble. They weren't ever gonna get out of where they were going, anyway."

Ted comes very close to saying what he's thinking, then stops and reminds himself that he's lucky to be riding in the front and not the back and follows Slavko and Steve up to the cab.

Steve is asleep in the rear compartment when they finally reach the old state highway, and Slavko slows the vehicle for the first time in fifteen hours. The route from the highway to Gower is onscreen, a mass of white with an electronic line showing where the road would be under the snow and estimating its depth, which averages 1.23 meters over the length of it, with a maximum of 2.81 meters.

"Hoping to sneak in without attracting undue attention, are we?" Slavko asks.

"What makes you say that?"

"You've got Chinese money but using ground transport, which suggests problems with your credentials."

"Oh."

"None of my business, of course..." Slavko trails off in anticipation of a clarification.

Ted doesn't respond. He's restless, sick of their offhand cruelty, and ready to hop out in his Chinese foul weather gear.

"It's been a pleasure having you aboard, Mr. Elder," Slavko says, extending his hand, once the vehicle has come to a full stop. "I hope you've gained some useful insight into the spending of your tax dollars."

Ted puts his helmet on, seals it and waves goodbye. When the door pops loose he pushes it open and steps backward down the ladder and onto a meter of snow, into which he sinks halfway before the door closes again and the truck pulls slowly out.

As the evening sky darkens he follows the road without much difficulty for an hour or more before the cozy warmth of the suit has his eyelids at half-staff. He opens the helmet and knocks back a shot of Noxadrene, courtesy of Steve, who also kindly gave him a couple of sealed shots of Diamorphidone right before hitting the cot himself. Without coming right out and saying that narcotics made him nervous, and not just for legal reasons, Ted said "I never need anything to help me sleep," and tried to hand back the sealed plastic cups.

"You will for a couple nights after you try the Noxadrene." As Steve seemed an authority on the pharmaceutical manipulation of the sleep cycle, Ted held on to them.

With the rapid kicking-in of the Noxadrene, his senses perk up, and the clumsiness of the foul weather gear becomes much more annoying. Though tempted to take the helmet off he's sufficiently in his right mind to know he can't. Every breath he takes in sounds like a cyclone and that warm air starts feeling prickly and dry on his hypersensitive skin. The whole scene before him seems brighter, whether it's an effect of the fully risen moon shining through an open patch in the cloud cover onto the snow or the influence of the speed on his optical nerves, and he begins trudging forward at a faster pace, which he finds improves the performance of the snowshoes. He makes a game of it, trying to see how close to the top of the mantle he can stay, and he pretends he's floating several feet above the ground, finally almost skiing over the surface of the snow.

Shortly after sunrise—such as it is, the sky still low and dark, with only a slightly brighter gray to indicate the coming of day—he consumes three energy bars, chocolate caramel flavor, opening the helmet's visor briefly and biting off as much bar as he can manage so as to minimize the amount of warm air lost. He marvels that he's only hungry and not exhausted after thirteen hours of walking, and he credits the Noxadrene with a complete lack of boredom as well. The shapes of the snowdrifts are endlessly fascinating, as are his attempts to picture all the various possibilities of the coming reunion with his wife and son. These range from the heartwarming to the very, very disturbing, but they all hold his interest and without causing him undue anxiety.

Based on long-ago experiments with less pharmaceutically pure forms of amphetamines, Ted's instinct is that the coming down is going to be a real sphincter-snapper, despite Steve's assurances that this stuff is new-generation, government-issued stuff and therefore as gentle on the system as cold medicine or boner pills. But he's got the Diamorphidone for that first night of sleep, so maybe Steve's right. It's been many years since he last overindulged in any such thing, and drugs are one of those rare things that have actually improved over the decades.

It's six in the evening when Ted crosses into Gower, and he sees no evidence of activity. There are a few dim lights on in the houses, but there's no one visible out of doors. He thinks of

Durango, happily connected to the Big Grid, and walking along a snowy street at night and seeing lights in all the windows there like when he was young.

Past Consuela's, he spots someone and steps into a doorway. Not that he has anything to hide, but there are people in town who don't like him, and others who do but are too naive to understand why he might want to keep his presence quiet. The figure nears, and for a few seconds he thinks there may be two of them, because he hears a woman's voice.

She's alone. "Hello, Ted," the woman says when she reaches the doorway, appraising him with a frankly disapproving twist of that perfectly smooth upper lip.

"Hi, Darla." He pulls off the helmet without asking or even wondering how she recognizes him.

"You better get ready to eat a whole lot of pussy when you get home, Brainiac, 'cause what I hear is Stacey's real mad."

He's absurdly happy to hear that slurpy rasp of hers, even to feel the flecks of spittle landing on his cheek.

"Where the hell you been? You got any idea what's been going on with your wife since you left town?"

He can imagine, but he doesn't especially care to hear it from Darla. "How are you, anyway?"

"Freezing my titties off. Man. I can't believe all these pussies staying inside, though. Remember when this used to be a fucking ski town? You think Jack Nicholson or Warren Beatty would have stayed inside the lodge because of a little snow? Shit, no. You and me are about the only two left in this town that still know how to party hearty. And Liz, too."

"Liz Glaspie?" He has some trouble picturing the vet's wife partying with Darla.

"God, can you picture that? A foursome with me and Liz and Jack and Warren." She shakes her head and cackles, that long, blonde hair whipping back and forth like in an old shampoo commercial and stopping to frame those rheumy red eyes and leather-tanned face. "Don't worry, Ted, Jack'll let you have sloppy seconds on me and Liz."

"Okay, Darla. I guess I'd better head for home."

"Be seeing you."

His face and neck are considerably stimulated by the cold wind, whose bite is considerably less savage than he would have imagined an hour ago. The breeze insinuates itself underneath his eyelids and sweeps over the tops of his eyeballs on its way to cooling his overheated brain. Or is that the Noxadrene? He decides to leave the helmet off for the rest of the short walk to Stacey's ranch, which he has never yet managed to start thinking of as his own. Probably just as well. She may have already divorced him, and if that's the case he can't blame her.

By the time he's in sight of the ranch house he's had to put the helmet back on since his hair was freezing in chunks, making him worry that it might snap off at the roots and leave him with unsightly bald patches. A lamp is on in the living room, as well as several others scattered through the house; given the pitiful amount of sunlight the house must have received for the last few days that means she's upgraded the solar system since he's been gone.

He calculates the kilowatt storage capacity of two or three new Thomson 390 Novapiles installed in tandem with a couple of GE molybdenum cells on the roof, in much the same way he started half-consciously rejiggering the filtration specs for the Taipei desalinization plant earlier in the day, the mathematical part of his brain working so fast he isn't conscious of any actual, conscious reckoning.

Good stuff, this Noxadrene.

On the porch he hears voices, male and female, of indeterminate number and identity. He raps hard and the voices stop until the door opens and Stacey stares at him in what looks to him like panic. He steps inside without her inviting him, precisely, and finds Buddy rising from the couch, pulling a nasty looking electrical zapper of a type Ted doesn't recognize from his vest pocket. It takes him a second to understand that they don't know who he is, and, laughing at the silly misunderstanding, he unlocks and removes the helmet. Buddy drops back down onto the couch, and Stacey turns and slumps against the wall.

"Jesus Christ. What the fuck are you doing here?"

"Honey, I'm home," he says, bright and high, and waits for a laugh that doesn't materialize. Stacey's been crying for a while by the looks of it, and her face is drawn and slick with sweat. She stares at him like he's a ghost.

He turns to Buddy. "I got your payment codes all ready for you. Bet you thought I'd skipped on you, didn't you?"

To Ted's bafflement the big man's attitude doesn't improve with this good and surely unexpected news. Buddy shakes his head and pinches the bridge of his nose. "Cole's gone," he says.

"He took a muni snowmobile and went down to the old Purdy mine pit."

"In *this* snow?" Surely this is the drugs playing him for a fool. He can't imagine his son getting there on his own, not even in the summer.

"I want Buddy to drive the Sno-Baby down there and get him," Stacey says.

"You're sick," Buddy says. "I'm not leaving you."

"Take the Sno-Baby. It won't take that long. What's the city even have it for if not for rescue operations?"

"It'll only take me up to the access road. After that it's on foot."

The Noxadrene has switched off his internal censor, and there's something Ted wants to get out of the way. "You guys have been fucking, right?" he says. Sick as she looks, Stacey eyes him with such threatening, violent contempt that he feels compelled to add, "That's cool, just trying to get the lay of the land here."

His hands start tingling and inside the thermal pocket of the suit he fingers the three plastic canisters he has left, two Diamorphidones and a Noxadrene. For the first time he's conscious of a bone-weariness in his body and a corresponding desire to collapse into what for a while used to be his bed. He's listening to Buddy and Stacey and trying to figure out whether he can risk another dose of Noxadrene without having bought a day's sleep with the Diamorphidone, only half-comprehending their confusing tale of some sexy biologist the boy's decided to go and rescue in the mountains.

They argue about other potential rescuers and caretakers and discuss the brutal logistics of what is bound under the best of circumstances to be a dangerous and time-consuming effort. Ted knows, though, what the outcome of all this is going to be, lethal dosage of Noxadrene or no, and so he cracks open the speed, downs it in a gulp and holds out his hands for the keys to the Sno-Baby.

16

HAVING HEARD A HIGH, KEENING WAIL that sounded vaguely like her own name, Bridget sticks her head through the secondary flap, and peering out with the greatest of caution she hears it again, this time unmistakably.

"Cole?" she yells back, certain she's hallucinating. She steps back inside the warmth of the tent and puts on her weather gear, then trudges out to find him waiting politely as if about to knock on the canvas, completely bundled in synthetics except for his eyes and nose.

"I came to make sure you were okay." The part of his face that's visible is a violent scarlet, and she pushes him into the tent. He sits down onto her inflatable chair and falls into an immediate, deep and—to Bridget's eye—untroubled sleep. Once the hat and the muffler and the stocking cap are removed the skin around the boy's eyes doesn't look so bad, the redness apparently from the cold rather than the noxious air around the Pit.

After an hour's slumber his redness dissipates and her fears of frostbite along with it. She spends a few minutes watching him snore and thinking how completely a few days without electronic stimulation alters what one finds entertaining. He's huskier than he was at the beginning of the season, and his face a little squarer, less a little boy's. She can't put her finger on why this makes her sad. She knows the change in him isn't something that happened over the four days she's been gone, but she certainly didn't take any notice of it before.

When he awakens an hour after that she asks him what he's doing there.

"Stacey was saying you weren't expecting any snow this early and how you don't have any cold weather gear."

"I can't believe Stacey let you do this."

He opens them again and looks down at the tent floor. "Well, she didn't, exactly. She was trying to get Buddy to do it but I knew he never would."

"*Jesus*, Cole." She touches his hair at the temple and the red returns to his face in a wave. "You shouldn't have done that."

"You're not from around here. I was afraid you might freeze." His face remains stoic, though his voice is straining. "I brought you some food," he says, opening his backpack. Inside are sandwiches and hardboiled eggs, their shells crystalline with frost.

"How about we let those things thaw a little bit." She opens up a can of dry roasted peanuts and puts them in Cole's hands. "Rex left me some elk meat but I don't know how to defrost it properly.

I guess he thought I was camped here for the winter, which I may be, if this doesn't let up."

"You can't," Cole says. "I had to leave the snowmobile down on the county road but we could get to it in a day."

"I'm surprised the snowmobile got you here at all."

"It started getting hard to drive last couple miles."

"And now it'll be carrying two."

"You can't stay all winter here. People die that way."

"You're right, I have to get you back home, don't I? So it's probably a good thing you showed up."

"Definitely is," he says.

"Okay, let's get some sleep and we'll pack up and go in the morning as soon as it's light."

Thirty hours later they're huddled together in a crude, hand-carved ice cave at the fork in the road that leads to the county road, where they stopped in exhaustion five hours ago. The snow and wind started up again in full force an hour after they broke camp, and their progress has been disastrously slow. She can't move as quickly through the snow as the boy, who has gallantly hung back with her, and half an hour after dusk they stopped here. The weather won't let them pitch the tent, and after the ordeal of digging the cave out of an enormous drift beneath an immense hemlock they're ready to give up. They crawled into a single sleeping bag to conserve warmth, having removed only boots and outer coats.

As she lies there in the darkness trying to drift off to sleep thoughts come unbidden to her mind of all manner of frozen deaths. An image from a documentary she saw in middle school of a frozen mountaineer, found on Everest fifty or sixty years after his demise, intrudes into her consciousness, and she tries to recall whether he died of a fall or from hypothermia. In the odd way that extreme situations focus the brain, she finds that scraps of information long-ignored have in fact clung to her memory. First to pop up is the disturbing fact that the intrepid Scott of the Antarctic actually perished there along with his men. Ah, but Amundsen lived to conquer the South Pole, didn't he? And then her subconscious provides another piece of disturbing trivia she wouldn't have been able to call up deliberately for any price: that Amundsen disappeared in the frozen wastes of the north a few years later.

She tries to silently recite "She Walks in Beauty," which she memorized as an undergraduate, but the thought of Byron leads to thoughts of Shelley, and then of Mary Shelley and finally, inevitably, to the horrible Arctic finale of *Frankenstein*.

My God, she's going to die out here out of her own sheer heedlessness, and so is this boy. If she'd acted like a reasonable adult he'd be safe and warm at home.

"Cole? What do you know about cold weather camping?" she says, unsure whether he's still awake.

"Not too much."

"I think I remember something about how you're not supposed to get into the sleeping bag when it's below freezing with your clothes on."

He says nothing, just breathes through his mouth, and his face is turned away from hers. Being aware of the boy's adolescent fixation on her she hates to bring this up, but she's not willing to die for the principle.

"It's something about sweating in the sleeping bag, and the sweat freezing on your clothes later and killing you while you sleep."

Still no answer from the boy, whose shoulders are noticeably hunched.

"Ever heard anything like that?" After another moment's silence comes a distinctly rueful *no*.

The pad under the bag is thin but the bag is thick and warm, made out of a Prylene blend, and for a few minutes after she turns the lamp off all she can hear is the consistent cracking of branches as they snap under the weight of the ice and snow, varying in pitch according to the thickness of the wood. After one *basso profundo* boom she worries for a minute about a tree coming down and crushing them, but before she's had a chance to reason the fear away she's asleep.

It's another noise that awakens her shortly after dawn, a huffing, almost choking sound that takes a second to take shape in her mind as breathing. She cranes her neck for a look at Cole, his eyes closed and his mouth lolling open.

Though she's half convinced it's Rex again, she pulls herself halfway out of the bag and opens a side pocket of her backpack, takes out the taser, and holds it at the ready.

Cole stirs, murmurs, and she shushes him, but he's only half-awake, and the sight of her sitting up from the sleeping bag draws from him something like a coyote's howl. He's halfway out of the bag himself when the breathing takes on a louder, more raucous tone, and a shadow darkens the entrance to the shelter. Goggled eyes appear at the opening as Bridget screams and sparks the taser, and Cole screams an octave higher.

The man pulls his goggles down to reveal a pair of red-veined vitrea. "Dr. McCallum, I presume," he says, sounding like a grizzly trying to speak. Bridget doesn't power the bear zapper down until Cole yells "Dad!" and climbs out of the bag to embrace him.

17

THEY SIT SCOWLING AT ONE ANOTHER over a game of crazy eights. Leo remembers playing it when he was little and not liking it, but it's the only game the two of them know the rules to besides checkers, at which Buddy cheats. Not that this surprises Leo, but it's tiring having to keep one eye on the board for the whole twenty minutes it takes to beat him. He suspects that some of Buddy's grumpy demeanor stems from the reappearance of his mother's current husband and his fear of being replaced in her affections by a more legitimate claimant.

His mother, ailing in her room, has her own clouding effect on their mood. The vet has been sent for, and this time Buddy has made a special request for the real doctor from the mine. This looks like a reprise of whatever she had a few weeks back, what Glaspie called appendicitis, and Leo is concerned that a second round of antibiotics will be useless against a bacterium made resistant by exposure to the first.

Every few minutes Buddy curses the insufficient battery power on the house's solar array, which Stacey refused to let him augment for free with another set of Daewoo Molybdenum TruLasts. The extras would have stored enough supplementary power even on the bleakest, grayest day that he would have been able to turn on a lamp to see his goddamn cards without worrying about the fridge conking out or the sump flooding or the land line failing.

"Can't see a fucking thing. Should have brought over a flashlight."

"You hear from the mine yet?"

"There's no signal."

"There might be from your office."

"There's no signal, Leo, if it might make the slightest fucking difference don't you think I'd be over there right now?"

He does know that, he just wishes Buddy would leave because Buddy's making him more antsy than he already would be. "Fuck this, you're cheating again." He gets up and looks in on his mother. "Still sleeping," he says. It's three in the afternoon and outside it looks like twilight, the snow coming down again wet and messy. He sees something coming in from the county road, a light bouncing too much to be mounted on a vehicle, even in the snow. Not the mine doc, then, but it might be Glaspie, which is better than nothing.

"Buddy. Someone coming." He suits up to assist whoever it is and stomps out into the murky gray afternoon. The snow is up to mid-thigh where he stands.

"Dr. Glaspie?" he yells, though the vehicle is moving too fast for anything the old man might be driving.

"It's us," he hears Cole yell back, whose return will do more for his mother than anything old Glaspie could.

By early evening the three adventurers are asleep, Bridget in the guest room and Ted sharing Cole's room, sleeping in a bag on the floor and having only managed to nod off after the application of some ungodly government-issue sleeping potion.

Buddy has started on his way back to the office, several hours distant now even on the snowmobile, to try and get a call through to the mine. He's promised that if he doesn't get through on the phone he's going to fire up the Sno-Baby and head over to the mine himself. "And I'm going to be armed, and if the little fucker doesn't want to come along I'll force him."

This was pure bravado—the mine is a maximum security installation—but Leo appreciates the spirit in which it was offered. He's drinking a cup of chicory when he hears the whinnying of Cole's fat pony loud enough to carry over the wind. Who knows if anyone's remembered in the midst of all this to take care of her? It takes him five minutes to get properly bundled for a pro-longed outdoor stint and another ten to figure out where Cole keeps the food and grooming equipment. By this time the pony is pounding its hooves and braying at him, and he talks to it as he brushes, finally managing to calm it down. Or maybe it's the food. He worries for a minute about the stable not being warm enough, until he looks down at the animal's swollen abdomen. It looks like a Mongol's mount, bred for the Siberian steppes, belly to the ground like an old-time Angus. It's completely calm now and as indifferent to him as always.

Leo fights his way through the drifts back to the cabin, where he sits awake until nine or so waiting for Buddy to get back. Then he spreads some sheets over the couch and goes to sleep.

In the morning the sky is blue, the snow on the ground blinding, and though there are immense storm clouds in the distance over the mountains Leo feels as if spring has arrived in early September. His mother isn't much different, though she cries when Cole comes in to see her. This embarrasses the boy, who nonetheless hugs her back. Bridget spends some time with her, too, though his mother is too weak to engage in conversation. Around noon Doctor Glaspie arrives on a snowmobile and examines Stacey with an air of helpless grief.

"I don't know what to tell you, boy," he says. "Maybe I got it wrong the first time. Buddy's out trying to bring the mine doctor in, but who knows if he'll come. If he doesn't there's nothing I can do besides another course of antibiotics."

"Why don't you start that now?"

"Have to wait and see what the other doctor says. If Buddy comes back alone at least he'll have the doc's advice and presumably some medicine."

In the early afternoon Bridget asks Leo to accompany her up to Chouteau while she does a follow-up report on her summer's work. They walk most of the way in high-stepping silence, stopping to eat a couple of energy bars at the base of the foothill, almost an hour from the front door. Even if they weren't laboring too hard for a conversation he wouldn't be in a talking mood. How is he supposed to admit that while his barely pubescent seventeen-year-old stepbrother was sneaking off in a blizzard to bring her back to what passes for civilization, he sat watching the snow pile up outside his warm house without Bridget ever crossing his mind?

Each of them carries a snow shovel for especially deep drifts, and by the time they reach the plateau they're ready to drop from the digging and the climb. It's late afternoon by now, and they stop again. It's still bright blue overhead, but to the east the sky is dark with immense billowy thunderheads, and neither of them speaks.

Once the terrain is level the going is easier, the drifts more navigable, and the pond is in sight within half an hour. He leans against the trunk of an ancient dead aspen and watches her go about her work, wonders what would happen if she decided to stay here or if he were to follow her to Boulder. Neither prospect seems likely, but worse things could happen. His mother's been on a kick lately telling him there's no future in Gower. Maybe she's right.

When they get back down to the house Buddy's sitting in the cab of the Sno-Baby with the windows sealed and darkened, and all Leo can see is his silhouette. He knocks on the door, but Buddy doesn't respond. The front door to the house opens, and Dr. Glaspie steps outside with a stricken look on his sagging, florid face. His mouth opens as if to speak, but something stops him and he covers his mouth.

A man he assumes is the mine doctor comes out of the bathroom with wet hands. "What's going on?" he asks.

"Are you the other son?" His gray hair is buzzed short, with sideburns down to the edge of his jaw.

He looks at Cole, who stands by the stairs staring down at his boots, eyes red, then back at Leo with a raised eyebrow. Cole hop-stomps up the stairs, snorting back snot, then slams his door.

The doctor sits down on the other end of the couch. He speaks slowly and precisely, in the manner of a technician accustomed to explaining things to dimwitted laymen. "Mister Elder—"

"My name's Hayden. Leo Hayden."

The doctor shrugs. "Your mother is suffering from Mendoza's Syndrome."

"I thought it was her appendix."

"So did that veterinarian. He was so zoned out when I got here Mrs. Elder's husband thought he'd had a stroke. I understand his being upset about the misdiagnosis, but I don't imagine he sees a lot of Mendoza's amongst the cats and the goats. You may want to keep an eye on him, I shot him up with a pretty powerful anti-anxiety, antidepressant cocktail."

"What's Mendoza's Syndrome?"

Caught off guard, the doctor stiffens, looks up at the ceiling and then down at the floor before answering. "It's a rare toxic reaction to certain...erectile hallucinogens."

"Why would Stacey be taking boner pills?" Bridget asks.

"She didn't, his honor the mayor did. Some of these compounds produce toxins in certain individuals. Usually it's the man who suffers, really bad penile pain, and I'm talking from personal experience here." The doctor pauses and lowers his voice. "Feels like someone's using your John Henry for a pincushion. Rarely we see cases where the toxin causes no pain but the concentration in the seminal fluid is so powerful that it can make the partner quite sick. There've been a handful of fatalities. The mayor tells me he's been experimenting with Flutril and Priapsipone and a couple of others, too."

"Aren't they against the law?"

"Come on. BoPharma's been manufacturing Priapsipone, for one, under the table for about three years. The President of the United States uses it, is what I hear."

"Goddamn Buddy." Despite himself, Leo feels a little twinge of pity for his former stepdad.

"I gather her husband just got home from a long absence. Really wanted to kill the mayor when he found out what happened, but I got him to opt for sedation instead."

"Did you sedate him or did he take the other dose of Diamorphidone?" Bridget asks.

The doctor glances sidelong at her without moving his head. "The latter," he says. He moves his entire body sideways to get a better look, and it seems to Leo that the man's neck won't move. "You're not from here," he says to Bridget. "You're the herpetologist."

"How did you know?"

"Lot of talk about you and your project. People on the state level." He sticks out his hand to shake. "Randy Schmick, M.D." He turns his whole stiff body to face her directly, squinting. "You're going to own a piece of the rights to whatever comes out of there. I guess that's the end of fieldwork for you."

"Wait a minute," Leo says. "How do you treat this Mendoza's Syndrome?"

"Strictly palliative."

"What's that mean?"

"It means we make her as comfortable as we can until she recovers...or dies. I gather this happened once before and she pulled through. Let's hope that's the case again."

An hour later the doctor is in the Sno-Baby's passenger seat, with Bridget in the jumpseat, watching a new snowfall coming down, laying a fresh powdery layer over the older frozen crust. The experience of riding in a vehicle ten feet above the ground is new to her, and she leans forward to get a better look at the blurred shower of snow in the high beams.

"This is the kind of snowstorm I loved when I was little. They always had to close school for days afterward. Wichita was never prepared for a heavy snow, even after they started coming winter after winter. Never had enough snowplows."

"What about *No Town Left Behind?*" Dr. Schmick asks.

"The town was getting deeper and deeper in the red every year so it didn't qualify. I know it's bad, but a good heavy snow like this still gives me a thrill, even after four years in Boulder."

Leo is content to let the two of them talk while he concentrates on the purely visual and neuromuscular task of keeping the Sno-Baby upright and on the road, trying not to think about his Mom. Within sight of the mine Dr. Schmick is telling them the story of how he ended up having his spine surgically fused, the result of a drunken fall into an open pit. "Had to chopper me to Denver. This was a few years ago, when Denver still had a couple good hospitals. I almost lost the job, but I know where all the bodies are buried at Lightnin' Queen, so they let it pass."

As the Sno-Baby nears the mine compound a glow becomes visible over the trees, and half a mile from the checkpoint the first brightly illuminated warning sign appears.

"You guys must be packing more panels down there than the whole town of Gower," Leo says. "This kind of weather, everything in Gower gets dim after a couple days."

The doctor laughs. "Panels? Come on."

"What, then? Some kind of dish collector?"

"You think we can power a big mining and refining operation with solar? Never mind the fact that if we didn't have twenty-four hour entertainment for those miners we'd have to work them at gunpoint."

This is the evening's second disconnect from Leo's accepted version of reality. "You're on the Big Grid?"

"Whoops." After a moment's thought he tries to turn again toward Leo, then settles for looking out the corner of his eye.

"If the mine's on it, why isn't Gower? Couldn't they just extend it another eight miles?"

"Sure, if your mayor wasn't the local solar panel dealer. Anyway, it was one of the conditions the last time we negotiated the royalty agreement."

"How come I never heard about any of this from any of the

miners?"

"The miners we let out of the compound are a bunch of Eastern European rubes who barely speak English, and they don't know the difference. The rest of us do our R and R at the executive facilities onsite, which beat the hell out of anything you've got in town."

Leo spends the rest of the drive wondering how he might wrangle a job at the Lightnin' Queen but keeps quiet. At the mine's gates he and Bridget are refused admittance, and the security guard keeps his weapon trained on Leo until the doctor is safely behind the locked gate. By now the snow has slowed.

Bridget breaks the silence after they hit a log on what turns out not to have been the road after all. "How often do you drive this thing?"

"Never. Maybe once every two or three years. Sorry."

"That's okay, I wouldn't be able to do it at all."

He manages to get the Sno-Baby back on the road, trying to act as though it's second nature to him. "I guess you're probably wondering why I didn't come get you."

She looks surprised. "I hadn't thought about it."

"I didn't hear you were missing until I got to the house because my Mom was sick, and Buddy told me Cole was missing. By that time Ted was on his way, so..."

"Forget it."

"Yeah, but I knew you were out there and I knew we were in the middle of the first big snow of the year. I never connected the two thoughts."

"I don't care." She really doesn't seem to give a damn.

The road is plainer now, a blank path between the trees, and Leo calms a little. The tension in his shoulders is almost painful, and he wishes he'd asked the doctor for a relaxant.

The house is dark when they pull up. Inside they pad up the stairs in their socks, and Leo pushes the door to the guest room open slowly. "Ted?" Bridget says.

He stirs on the bed, mumbling, and she calls his name again. Then the bedside light comes on, pale and orange and diffuse, and Dr. Glaspie squints up at them. His face a picture of nirvana, Glaspie swings his legs over the side of the bed and grabs his knees with big muscular hands, oblivious to the fact that his penis is hanging out the fly of his boxers, equine in scale even in its flaccid nocturnal state. Bridget lets out a startled, high-pitched giggle at the sight of it and looks up at the ceiling, her already pink cheeks going so red so fast Leo thinks she may burst a vessel.

"Sorry to wake you, we thought this was where Ted was sleeping."

"I believe he's in the boy's room," the doctor says. This is the first time Leo has had occasion to note the grayness of his incisors, the lowers peglike from decades of night-grinding, and this combination of unrestored teeth, stubbornly un-regenerated scalp, and his sudden Buddha nature lend him an air of ancient, infallible wisdom. "What keeps you children up at this hour?"

"Took the doctor back to the mine," Leo says.

"A good sawbones, that doctor. Makes me see the folly of pretending to be one myself. The foolish pride of it." He's still grinning, apparently amused at this sudden self-awareness. "He shot me up with a hell of a potion and I am one relaxed son of a bitch."

Leo shoots Bridget what he means to be a furtive glance but they hold each other's gaze for a long beat before turning back to the old man.

"I know, everybody thinks I don't know any cuss words. I'm just not scared of them anymore. Usually I'm scared of everything," he says. "I wish I'd discovered this stuff thirty years ago. Schmick left me enough to last until the next TarMart shipment."

"That's great, Dr. Glaspie," Bridget says.

"Call me Eddie, please."

"Eddie."

"You know what, Leo? If your Mom doesn't pull through I'm going to slice Buddy's balls right out of his ballsack." He crawls back under the covers and flips off the lamp.

18

REX KEEPS THE SKULL WITH THE ANTLERS on a shelf above his taxidermy bench as a talisman and an aid to concentration, finding it particularly useful at times like these when confronted with multiple, thorny, seemingly unrelated problems. When he found it a decade ago he took it for that of a holy man, maybe a Ute, with some kind of hunting medicine; the antlers were short and knobby and without points, but they sure looked like a buck's springtime buds. His brother Danny called it the *mantelope* and said back in the old days you could have made postcards of it to sell to tourists.

Rex took it into town one day to show Doctor Edwin Glaspie, D.V.M., and asked him if it was possible to cross a human and a deer. Glaspie, who to Rex's hurt and bafflement has always made plain his contempt for and fear of all things Daggett, had a goddamned shit fit right there in his examination room and started quoting Bible verses about not laying down with animals. A light came on in Rex's mind and he understood then that it had been a stupid question, since his cousin Wink had been fucking barn animals of every description since his first dickhairs sprouted without ever once siring a litter of little chimerical Daggetts.

"What's the story on them antlers, then?" he said, handing the yellow-brown thing to the old vet, who examined it with a scowl and pronounced it a forgery.

"What's the idea there?" Rex asked.

"A forgery. A deliberate fake."

"I know what it means, I just don't know what's the idea faking something like this and then just leaving it. Looks like it's been there a long time, don't it?"

"Mr. Daggett, sometimes things are put here on Earth to test our faith. I don't know who put it there or why, but human beings and animals cannot interbreed."

A year later when he had to go into Boulder to get his half-brother Jimmy's jaw rebuilt he brought the skull with him. At the college he got passed around from department to department— one professor of American Studies told him if the skull was Indian he'd have to return it to the Bureau of Indian Affairs for repatria-tion, at which suggestion Rex offered to give the skull a one-way trip up the wrong end of the professor's alimentary canal, antlers and all—until he reached a kindly lady in the anthropology depart-ment who informed him that the skull looked to her like a white person's, probably male and probably not much over twenty.

"What about the antlers?"

"They're not really antlers. See, this is bone here, growing right out of the skull, even though it has that kind of knobby look antlers have. I'm guessing this was a person with a great deal of genetic trouble."

"Uh-huh."

"Where did you find it?"

"Boward County."

The old lady's eyebrows shot upwards. She was stooped over and white-haired in a way Rex hadn't seen in a while, the way his great-grandmother used to look, but she was fuller of piss and vinegar than a lot of people Rex's age. "Anywhere near Purdy? Played-out copper mine?"

"Pretty close. Up the side of the mountain to the pit."

"That's an old Superfund site. No wonder."

"What's that mean?"

She handed the skull back to him with a grin that revealed a mouthful of yellow teeth with sparkling white caps. "Means you probably ought to get rid of it."

The mystery was solved a couple of years later when his cousin Buck dropped in for a visit. Wiry and mean and old, Buck had been around when there were still people living at Purdy, and though he'd never seen the man alive he recognized the skull right away.

"That's Neely Bowen's baby brother right there. You dig up the poor sumbitch's grave, boy?"

"Found it up near Purdy. Neely Bowen hasn't got any brother and never did have."

"Sure as hell used to. He was an idiot, came out with bumps on his head looked like somebody'd coldcocked him. They kept him inside and nobody ever saw him, but all of us friends of Neely's knew about him. Family's all gone now except for Neely. Mind he don't find out you got his retard brother's skull on your fucking shelf."

Now Rex sits at his workbench staring into Neely's brother's eyesockets (Buck had drawn a blank as to the idiot's Christian name) and wondering what the hell these University people are going to do with that contaminated shitwater down at Purdy. *Cancer cure my sweet pink ass.* Going to grow giant farm animals so people in the city can get some meat for a change, and then there's going to be a whole nation full of imbeciles with horns coming out their foreheads. Which is probably just exactly what the government wants.

This is no small matter but lacks the urgency of the disposal problem. Sending the lady scientist down to Purdy was the right thing to do, Rex knows that, but he didn't anticipate her coming back with a bunch more scientists next year, nor did it occur to him that the state might want to stake a claim to such worthless land. And now word comes that Buddy Gallego is making a counterclaim on behalf of the county, all of which means that the land in that narrow little valley is going to be invaded by surveyors and geologists and who knows what kind of specialist, all of them posing threats to his pretty little cemetery. What would Neely's idiot brother tell him to do, if he could speak?

What would the mantelope do?

A knock comes at the door of the workshop and Lamar steps in. "Bother you for a second, Rex?"

He gestures toward the only other seat in the room, an ancient chair constructed out of buffalo horns and leather. Rex found the chair in an old ski lodge that had been looted of its other valuables.

"How's the girls doing?"

"They're just fine, thanks."

"Cabin not too small?" Before the girls arrived Lamar was staying in the house with most of the Daggetts; when they joined him Rex put them all up in the newest cabin he has, which Rex's own wife Raven and Ivan the hairdresser fixed up nice for them.

"No, not at all. The thing is, Gail has the girls doing schoolwork in the wintertime, normally."

"In the wintertime? When you can't even get to school?"

"The idea is to keep them far enough ahead that if they ever get the chance to go to college they won't have to catch up. School here doesn't teach most of what they'd need to know to survive in a real school."

"Okay." Having had almost none himself Rex reserves a great deal of respect for education, and he's dismayed to learn that the school at Gower isn't up to snuff; he's always been intimidated by its alumni, and this new knowledge makes him feel a little stupider than before.

"I was wondering if you could think up a way we could get some of Gail's books out of the house, if they're still there. I know it's a lot to ask, after all you've already done."

"Don't worry about it. Just tell me what it is we need to get and

I'll find out the lay of the land this afternoon. Got to go and see a man about delivering some meat."

In town Rex sees Doctor Glaspie and out of habit turns away, but the old man calls out to him with such disarming warmth that he relents and approaches. "Sad news, Rex," he says. "Isn't it?"

"What's that, sir?"

He puts his hand on Rex's shoulder. "You haven't heard, then? I hate to be the one to tell you, because I know you were friendly with her."

"With who?"

"Stacey Elder. Stacey Chouteau Hayden Gallego Elder, I guess, if you want to go back that far." The doctor seems tickled by this feat of memory, which makes Rex want to shake him.

"What's the matter with her?"

"Isn't it funny, I always thought the less of her for all that marrying. As if it was any of my damned business."

Distracted though he is by the doctor's use of even the mildest of curses, Rex is alarmed by the gist of the message the geezer's delivering so slowly. "Doctor Glaspie, you better tell me what's up with Mrs. Elder."

"She passed on this morning, Rex." His eyes go wet and sad very quickly, and he looks up at Rex in supplication, as if hoping Rex can make it not so anymore.

Rex finds it hard to swallow a large load of saliva that seems to have instantly materialized inside his mouth. "How?"

"Something called Mendoza's Syndrome. Seems it's a sort of pharmaceutical venereal disease."

"I never heard of it."

"Apparently his honor the mayor's use of a pharmaceutical aphrodisiac, or what the kids call a *boner pill*," he says, his wrinkly old eyes smiling for a second at the naughtiness of it, "caused a fatal toxic buildup in Stacey's body."

"Now hold on. Old Buddy did this to her?"

"In a manner of speaking. Or you could blame it on BoPharma, they're the ones who make it."

Rex nods, gorge rising, knuckles itching, teeth grinding. "They know this happens? They even have a name for it?"

"I suppose they do know. Apparently the manufacturing is under the table now."

"Ought to blow up the damn factory."

"Oh, but they do a world of good, too, Rex. Think of all the research they're doing right now, trying to cure the world's diseases. Think of the good works going on in those same labs."

He nods. He's not thinking about the labs, though, he's thinking about Stacey, about the pit, about his disposal problem, about his private little bone orchard.

"I hope your family's all well, Rex. I know sometimes I've judged you harshly, particularly your brother Danny, but you do good things for the people of this valley." The doctor puts a friendly hand to his shoulder and Rex wonders what exactly has gotten into the old coot. It's an improvement, whatever it is, but he doesn't quite seem like he's the same old doctor who's been giving him shit all these years.

It would be untrue to suggest that Rex has never been bothered by his brother's carnal tastes; the sort of behavior he has always indulged in could have gotten the boy killed without Rex's protection. But his brother is his brother, and Danny is a hell of a tracker and a hunter, cocksucking habit or no. The Plains Indians, Danny is fond of telling anyone who'll listen, treated his kind with respect and awe. Rex doesn't know if this is true or not, but he's come to believe that his brother comes by his ways honestly.

Funny what a man can get accustomed to. When Danny convinced him last year that Ivan the hairdresser was about to get hustled away to some kind of deprogramming camp—the kind where they walk in queer and walk out either pretending to be straight or not at all—they welcomed him up there at the compound and made him an honorary Daggett. Damned if Rex and the others haven't come to think of him as part of the family now, a full-fledged gay brother-in-law, which would have struck their mother as damned peculiar and their father as a public disgrace, and never mind what their grandfather would have done. But Danny's happy now in a way he wasn't before when he had to sneak into town to meet Ivan in the middle of the night, so fuck all those dead Daggetts who don't have to deal with the world anymore.

Danny isn't saying much as he and Rex move down the mountainside toward the graveyard, each carrying a hundred feet of coiled siphoning tube on his back. It's so cold anyway that it hurts your throat, not to mention the stench of the nearby pit, which even in the coldest times of the year gives off a smell that could peel the plates right off an armadillo.

Rex is thinking about Stacey Elder and getting madder and madder. She's been dead a whole day now. She was a good customer, but more than that she always treated him right, like a neighbor and not some crazy man living in the wilderness, the way some townspeople did. And she let him hunt on her property, on and offseason. The Daggetts will all be at the funeral tomorrow paying their respects.

The cemetery was of both brothers' making. Danny helped him dig the graves and carry the deceased and even said a prayer over the men they'd killed after the holes were filled back up, something Rex wouldn't have thought to do and which he resisted at the time, given that the deceased were a pack of security contractors who had frankly needed killing, the way some people do.

He was worried at the time that this might mark the end of the truce between him and the Feds, but the Feds seem to have decided that a bunch of dead contractors weren't worth a confrontation. Which is fine with Rex, because he likes the compound where it is right now, and the last time he had to move it was after a whole lot of shooting and he had to do it with his right leg shot up, an injury he's reminded of every time he takes a step on it, particularly when it's cold.

The digging itself isn't bad as he expected, since the ground up top hasn't been frozen long, and the disturbance is recent enough that the soil hasn't completely packed down again. There are seven graves, their contents pretty moldy and rotten, but the smell of the pit pretty much drowns out the odor, which makes him wonder whether the lady scientist wasn't on to something when she suggested he put on a respirator working around the pit.

The bodies go into gunnysacks, which the brothers toss side-handed onto the frozen surface of the pit, which isn't very thick and cracks as each one lands and spins across the surface toward the bubbling, liquid center, slipping under into the noxious brew. When all seven have gone under, precipitating an extra-frenzied bubbling and smoking at the surface, Rex joins the two lengths of uncoiled siphoning tube and sticks one end of it into the pit, cracking the frozen ice near the edge and nearly passing out from a good whiff from the nozzle. Then he takes from his pack the small underwater pump and connects the tube's far end to it and cuts a hole in the ice of the pond. It's hard cutting here—plain water freezes more readily than whatever's in the pit—but when he gets a good open spot there's no gas spewing up, so he supposes that's something.

A flick of the switch and he drops the pump into the pond, and swiftly the noxious liquid starts flowing from pit to pond, and he and Danny sit down for a technical discussion.

"How long before you figure the pit sludge kills everything in the pond?" he asks.

Danny looks at the pond and squints. "Water level's a little bit low. That's good, means we can pump a decent amount in without having to pump the water back out into the pit. Wish't we had a bigger pump."

"We don't, though."

"I imagine we'll have a good, toxic, flammable mixture in there by late tomorrow," Danny says.

"All right. Let's set them timers and fuck on off out of here."

19

COLE IS TRYING TO EXPLAIN to Gingie that if he'd been home instead of off rescuing Dr. McCallum then Buddy wouldn't have had done the poison sperm thing with Stacey that night and she'd be alive right now. Gingie lets out a long breath like she's thinking about a way to convince him that this isn't so, and he notices a stray nose hair vibrating in the stream.

They're seated on the couch and she's hugging him in an awkward way, because she's the county social worker but also a kind of shirt-tail relation, and he senses that she's having a hard time striking the right balance of familial affection and professional distance.

"Those pills have a cumulative effect. In other words it wasn't that particular night or that particular session of...of man-and-lady business. Probably it would have happened anyway the next time they..."

She's working hard to find an appropriate phrase, and it's all he can do not to pipe up with suggestions. She finally settles on "The next time they got together."

Nina is asleep in her grandmother's bed with Bee next to her, and Ted is outside making himself busy and avoiding his wife's family.

Stacey's body is gone; Bridget and Leo loaded her into the Sno-Baby and drove her into town, to Lamar's barber shop, though with Lamar gone there's some question as to who will prepare the body for burial. To Leo and Bee it doesn't seem to matter much, just as it wouldn't have mattered to their mother.

"Gingie? What are we going to do for food tomorrow?"

She pulls away, holds her head in her hands at the odd question. "If you're worried about who'll take care of you from now on, you know you can stay with me and Bee and Nina, right?"

"I don't need to with my Dad back. I mean food for the funeral."

"Oh," Gingie says, the tips of her right fingers moving up to her lower lip and pulling it down. The funeral will draw half the town and there will have to be food. "I guess that's on us, isn't it? Probably Bee and I will get something from Rex."

"I want to do the meat myself," he says.

To his great embarrassment her eyes get teary and she pulls him to her breast again, rubbing his shoulderblades. "What about the Hero Dogs, sweetie? What about the county festival?"

"Won't be any festival this year because of the snow and next year I'll be too old. Anyway I'm leaving with my Dad for China and I don't care about feeding the Hero Dogs anymore. I want to do it for Stacey."

"You know how to do it yourself?"

"Kind of. I was hoping my Dad and Juan would help."

"All right. When Bridget gets back with the Sno-Baby we'll all ride into town. Okay?"

"Okay."

Ted is chopping cordwood in the stable, and seeing him he looks so angry Cole doesn't know whether to interrupt or not. He supposes that his Dad sees every chunk of wood as Buddy's face, or maybe his belly.

The whole Buddy-as-instrument-of-death aspect of the situation is difficult for Cole, since he's always liked the mayor, even when Stacey was cheating on his Dad with him.

But knowing that Buddy intercoursed her to death for the sake of some kind of boner pill fills Cole with loathing. He's even mad at Bridget for trying to deceive him, keeping him out nights when Stacey and Buddy were meeting—even if he had been delighted to pretend he didn't understand the context of those nights, more than happy to assist in his father's cuckolding if it meant time spent alone, close to Bridget.

Mysti looks dispassionately at him with one big brown eye from her stall. Having been fed she's no longer interested in him. For a moment he wonders what it would have been like, winning the blue at County, earning the admiration of all the Ag kids and even the town kids, maybe getting some kind of scholarship like Bridget talked about.

And like one program replacing another on a screen, Cole allows himself to articulate the thing he's been most afraid of all summer, afraid even to imagine. It's there in his father's face as he attacks the cordwood and the splinters fly, that feeling of deep, humiliating betrayal leading to an inexpressible, disconsolate sorrow that's a hairsbreadth from murderous rage on the male emotional spectrum.

Did Leo risk his life in the middle of winter trying to rescue Bridget? Did Leo spend the summer running errands and keeping her company? Worshipping her? Leo did nothing, nothing at all, and the idea that she'd choose him when he clearly doesn't care about her one way or another is unbearable.

But he understands that, being seventeen years old, and looking younger at that, no other scenario was possible. He wills these atavistic emotions into abeyance, and when he's sure he's not going to break out into anymore tears he calls out to his father, who looks up from his chopping and wipes the sweat off of his forehead with the ragged sleeve of an old weather suit, looking like he's been caught at something. His mouth hangs open and he wipes a dribbling strand of saliva with that same filthy old sleeve.

"What's up?" his Dad says.

"Can you give me a hand with Mysti?"

The next morning Cole wakes up in Bee's living room before the sunrise. He suits up and crunches across the black snowy expanse of her yard, traverses the empty predawn streets of Gower, navigating mostly by memory, the sky so thick with cloudcover there's not even starlight to reflect off of the snow and light his way.

Main is still clogged with the stuff but Buddy has sworn it will be cleared by midafternoon for the funeral procession from Lamar's erstwhile barbershop to the cemetery. Cole knocks on the back door at the top of the stairs behind Consuela's, where Juan Stevens is already brewing a pot of the coffee he's released from his semi-secret private stash.

"Thought that was supposed to be for the funeral," he says.

"There's plenty left for that. Just thought you and I could have some before we get started. Big job ahead. More than one, in fact."

At the ancient Formica table in Juan's living quarters they drink the coffee black and mutter.

"Real sorry about Stacey. She was all right."

"Yeah," Cole says.

"Sorry for your Dad, too. Hear he made himself and Buddy a good little chunk of money with the Chinese."

"Don't know if Stacey would have come along with us to China."

"Still, nice if she'd've had the option."

Cole nods. He likes something about the taste of the coffee, something that's missing from the chicory he's been drinking his whole life. He feels his heart beating faster with a curious thrill akin to what he imagines drug fiends must feel.

"You sure you're up to this?" Juan asks.

"Yep. Have to do it."

"Okay, then, let's get started. Funeral's at five, people gonna be eating at six. We have to have everything ready."

They head down the fragile wooden backstairs and cross town

to the old Atchison barn, the air subarctic and the sky lightening from grayish black to blackish gray. In the near distance he can hear Mysti whinnying for her breakfast.

20

By six o'clock that night Stacey has been put into the ground—unembalmed, since the absent Lamar has for years been the town's undertaker as well as its barber—next to her mother and father. From the stage of the Opera House, the crowd of friends, colleagues and former students was worthy of a TarMart delivery day, and even the largest church in Gower would have had to turn mourners away—Dr. Glaspie gave an oration unlike any the assembled crowd had heard from him before, or from anyone, for that matter: *God was welcoming home one of His most beautiful creations and we should all be rejoicing with these reunited parts of the cosmic soul.* The doctor then expounded at some length about aspects of the afterlife that to many a mourner's ear didn't sound very orthodox, though it was generally agreed that it was a lovely eulogy.

While Ted and Cole and Bee and Buddy and Leo were lowering the casket into the ground Ted noticed a spot of dried blood on his son's shirtcuff, which he ignored. The boy and Juan had worked for nine hours getting the supper ready, and getting clean wasn't easy. Ted's head has not yet stopped buzzing from the past few days' zigzagging drug combinations, his rage against his ex-friend Buddy not yet supplanted by the grief that is surely about to lay him out flat.

The dinner, for family and a few invited friends only, is held at Consuela's. Seated at the head table with the widower and his son are Leo and Bee and Gingie and Nina, the Glaspies and Bridget. Buddy has been exiled to the second table next to Karen Ingelblad, an awkward situation since he dallied with her for several years before throwing her over for Stacey. Lena Gallego declined to accompany her husband to any of today's events, and barred her daughter from leaving the house as well. Going stag to a funeral is not the mayor's style, and afraid as he is that he'll start blubbering over the meal, Buddy forces himself to concentrate on Miss Ingelblad's lovely, graceful throat. That she refuses to acknowledge his presence he accepts as his due.

The room is filled with the smell of roasted meat, assertive enough to overpower any lingering trace of the restaurant's usual pleasant odors of cumin and oregano and canned tomatoes. The meat glistens on the plates. It's marbled perfectly and sends out as fragrant a bouquet as any beef or venison Cole has ever smelled, the cuts thick and rosy. Cole takes great pride in the faces of the diners, at the appreciative slowness of their chewing, of the way the food helps alleviate, in its small way, their sorrow. He's surprised when the doctor taps him on the wrist and says with a fond smile "You ought to be proud, boy," aware as he is of Dr. Glaspie's attitude toward that particular sin.

He catches Bridget watching him and his face reddens. She gives him a miniature, secret smile and toys with the quivering, translucent green glob on her plate next to her slice of roast. "I never heard of serving mint jelly with venison."

Dr. Glaspie laughs out loud with such unaccustomed delight it gives her a start. "Isn't venison."

"What is it, then?" Bridget asks.

"It's Mysti," he says.

She stops chewing for a second, then starts again, slowly. She likes it, and before she even knows she's doing it she's cutting herself another bite. "I don't believe I've ever eaten a horse before."

"A pony, to be precise. Properly raised and prepared, it can be a delicacy. And this one certainly is, thanks to Juan and young Mr. Elder. I must say, Cole, I'm pleased you decided not to feed it to those damned Hero Dogs. What a waste that would have been."

As the entire table registers the shock of the mild sacrilege that has just escaped the doctor, Bridget turns to Cole, not quite convinced she's not being kidded. "But you loved that pony."

He shrugs. "I worked real hard on her."

The doctor, still beaming, puts his hand on Cole's shoulder. "You're a city girl, Miss McCallum. Out in the country we don't grow so easily attached to animals."

She looks over at Liz Glaspie, who studies her husband with some concern, but not without a certain fond fascination. Seeing this new side of him, Bridget thinks she understands the connection between them a little better, and she tries hard not to picture him as she saw him the other night, naked and equine.

"This is some excellent filet mignon, baby," Darla says to old Brett McCaughey, fighting the urge to reach out and grab his long, braided soul patch, which bobs up and down as he chews.

"Isn't beef, Darla, it's horse."

"Fuck you, Brett, you don't know shit from shinola about cuisine. I know what I'm talking about, I used to get the filet all the time over at the Chateaubriand. I don't recall ever seeing you in any kind of higher class restaurant than Arthur Fuckin' Treacher's Fish and Chips."

"Horse."

"Filet. Fuckin'. Mignon." The obtuse stubbornness of the man infuriates her, but she guesses she could see getting it on with him later. She thinks warmly of all the times she's gotten laid after funerals. It's been a while, but it used to happen just about every time someone punched their ticket, something about the presence of death having always given Darla the urge to rut. "Hey, McCaughey, you ever make the beast with two backs anymore?"

"The what?"

"I'm asking when's the last time you got your ashes hauled." She gives her hair a toss and licks her lower lip.

Before he can answer Buddy snuffles over with a bottle of wine, his cheeks slick with unashamed tears and those big green eyes brimming with more. "This shit was Stacey's favorite and we're gonna drink the whole case up tonight in her honor." He pours four fingers into Darla's water glass and two into Brett's.

After steeling himself he maneuvers over to the head table with two full bottles and pours for the whole table except for Dr. Glaspie. Cole takes a swig and frowns appraisingly at Bridget. "Interesting," he says with a discerning frown, but she's looking past him at his father, gamely enduring a bear hug from Buddy.

"I'm sorry," Buddy sobs.

"It's okay, Buddy, keep pouring. That's what Stacey would have wanted," Ted says.

"Whole damn case was supposed to be a surprise for her. Shit, I can't even pour it right without her here. She always had to tell me whether I was supposed to pour it into a pitcher or just into a glass. Shit."

"It's all right, your honor," Dr. Glaspie says. "Give me a nice big dollop for Stacey, would you?"

Once again the table fixes on Dr. Glaspie. Buddy pours, and the doctor takes the water glass and sips, eyes closed. "2015. Think of that."

"That was a good year, Eddie," Liz says, and he kisses her full on the lips, mouths wide open. Liz giggles, then has to swat him hard on the arm, and when he disengages he's blushing as brightly as she is.

The old man stands and hefts the glass, tapping it with his knife, and as the room quiets down he takes a long sniff of the wine, so absorbed in it that a stranger never would have known he was a lifelong teetotaler taking his first glass. "Ladies and gentlemen, boys and girls, it is not usual or traditional to propose a toast at a funeral, but overwhelmed as I am with emotion at the loss of my friend I would like to propose one to the family, extended and nuclear, of Stacey Elder. May they prosper and multiply."

Buddy puts his hand on Ted's shoulder and whispers into his ear. "I never gave her this." He places a sealed envelope into Ted's hand.

"It's okay," Ted says, laying the envelope on the tabletop and thinking that if he weren't bound for a better life in China in a few days, if it weren't for his son, he might yield to the temptation of killing Buddy. He wishes he'd had the nerve to cheat his old friend out of at least a fraction of his Chinese desalinization royalties, and contents himself with the thought of his well-appointed Hong Kong lab and all the new ideas he's going to be chasing.

The door to the restaurant opens and four of the Daggetts enter. They shut it behind them before letting too much cold air in, and Rex speaks. Rex is the only one most of the assembled have ever heard speak, anyway.

"We're real sorry everybody we had to miss the funeral but it was more of a mess getting here than we thought."

They sit down with Darla and Brett McCaughey and, nodding their greetings, set out to eat meat killed for once by someone other than themselves.

Rex is guessing that not a single vertebrate will have survived the influx of the pit's liquid into the pond, whatever delicate balance of contaminants that allowed the tadpoles to develop and grow upset now by the toxic, ghastly potage he and Danny pumped into it. By his reckoning, remarkably accurate for a man who doesn't own a timepiece, the electronic countdown on the twin detonators is nearing its end, one of them attached to the rapidly effervescing and dissolving cadaver of a security contractor at the bottom of the pit, the other to a chunk of sandstone at the bottom of the lifeless pond.

The muffled boom gets a rise out of everyone at Consuela's except for the Daggetts, Darla, and Eddie Glaspie, all of whom go right on eating. Rex looks up as people begin filing to the window, and then to the door. He wipes his mouth and walks over to Bridget's table.

"I'm awful sorry," he says.

Bridget clears her throat, unsure why his condolences are being addressed to her rather than to the family of the deceased, nods and clears her throat. "She was a nice lady."

"You're right, she was. That ain't it, though. What I meant was I'm awful sorry about what I done to the pit."

"What do you mean?"

He gestures toward the door. She stands and follows him to it, and they step outside in the cold. In the distance, well over into the next range, a thick plume of orange smoke with sinister yellow highlights rises, with a daintier one next to it.

"You did that?" she asks, more confused than angry. "What happened?"

Rex squints at the smoke. "Reckon I might have miscalculated a little bit on the amount, there."

"Amount of what?"

"Explosive, Ma'am."

"It's on fire? Oh, Jesus, Rex." Her hand is covering her face below her eyes.

"Like I said, I'm real sorry about your work and all, but that shit up there is nasty as hell and it needed to get gotten rid of years ago, and the world doesn't need anymore goddamn boner pills like what killed Stacey Elder."

"Rex," she says, putting her palm on his chest. "Do you know what's in that smoke? Do you know what happens to those compounds when they burn?"

"Nuh-uh."

"I don't either, but I bet it's not good."

By now everybody is outside, most of them having put their coats on. Everybody jumps at the sound of another explosion, a deep, booming echo that hits a few seconds after the burst of flame from the mountaintop, obscuring the view of the pit valley with a plume of fire and smoke.

A mining company helicopter appears in the distance, heard before it's seen, and hovers high above the smoke for a few seconds before turning and flying back toward the mine.

"What the fuck is going on over there," Buddy says, having intuited that Rex had a hand in whatever has just gone wrong.

"Pit's burning off," Rex says. "Won't be no use to you now. Or anyone else."

"*Jumping Jesus,*" Buddy spits. "What are we supposed to do now?"

"Just enjoy the show, I guess."

Cole Elder looks around the mostly empty room—only Brett McCaughey, Darla and three of the Daggetts are still eating—and reaches for the envelope Buddy handed his father. It's addressed to Stacey, and for a moment he wrestles with the ethics of opening a dead person's mail. The better angels of his nature fail to convince and he tears it open, scanning with distaste through the mushy declarations of love that open the letter and fixing instead on the details of his father's genius, the government's lack of interest in his desalinization technology while simultaneously refusing a license to export.

> Under the circumstances I have no choice but to make my way to San Francisco and from there bribe my way on to a cargo container bound for Hong Kong. If I make it there alive I'll sell the work and make my way back here for you and Cole.

The mushy part picks up again at this point and runs for a nauseating three paragraphs before he gets serious again:

> You wouldn't have let me go, and you know that, and if you hate my guts for keeping you in the dark that's understandable. All I ask is for you to take care of Cole until I return. I've talked to Buddy about pulling strings to keep him out of the Armed Services but you know Buddy. Keep after him on that.

At this point comes more painfully abject stuff begging her to forgive him for deceiving her and a long, gooey finale.

Cole finds himself not at all sad about leaving the only home he's ever known. In China he'll go to school and make something of himself. He'll find Bridget somewhere, and some day, when he's too old for military service, he'll return to Gower with Bridget as his bride. By then the difference in their ages will be unimportant, and everything that matters will be better.

Cole wanders outside and watches without much curiosity the billowing, smoky pillars that seem to fascinate everyone else. His father puts a hand on his shoulder and clasps it, and Bridget, leaning against the wall, looks ready to collapse. The Daggetts watch without speaking, and the whole town stands there outside of Consuela's, in the streets and on the rooftops of Gower, hoping the wind doesn't shift.

ACKNOWLEDGMENTS

The author would like to thank Megan Abbott, Nicole Aragi, Jim Hanks, Jedidiah Ayres, David Hale Smith, Blake Crouch, and Augustino Patti.

The Concord Free Press thanks our family and friends—and our readers and supporters throughout the world.

The Concord Free Press is an experiment in publishing and community.

And now you're part of it.

This book is free. All we ask is that you give money to a group you support or someone in need. Where and how much you give—that's completely up to you. Just chart your donation at our website. Then—and we know this is the hard part—**pass your book along** to another reader so that the reading and giving can continue.

The Concord Free Press is about inspiring generosity. Thanks for yours.

Chart this book's progress and donations at:
www.concordfreepress.com.

YOUR BOOK IS #  566

Please sign your copy of *Rut*
before you pass it on.

1. _____

2. _____

3. _____

4. _____

5. _____

6. _____

7. _____

8. _____

9. _____

10. _____

Concord Free Press

CONCORD
FREE
PRESS